The Bounty Hunter's Sister

Brides of Cedar Falls, Book #3

Jo Grafford, writing as Jovie Grace

JG
Press

SECOND EDITION: This book was originally part of the Silverpines Series. It has since been rewritten and expanded to be part of the **Brides of Cedar Falls Series** — uplifting historical romance full of faith, hope, love, and cowboys!

ISBN: 978-1-63907-066-4

Acknowledgments

Thanks so much to my editor, Cathleen Weaver, and an enormous thank you to my beta readers — J. Sherlock, Auntie Em, and Mahasani. I also want to give a shout out to my Cuppa Jo Readers on Facebook. Thank you for reading and loving my books!

For more about my books —>

Follow on Bookbub
https://www.bookbub.com/authors/jovie-grace

Follow on Amazon
https://www.amazon.com/author/joviegrace

Read FREE Bonus Stories
https://www.JoGrafford.com/bonuscontent

Join Cuppa Jo Readers
https://www.facebook.com/groups/CuppaJoReaders

Chapter 1: Sewing Unrest

January, 1867

Charity Powers knew she couldn't hide in the guest room forever, though it was tempting. The plush window seat cushion she was perched on was so comfortable that she could easily remain there for hours. Only a few feet away, the fire on the hearth was blasting enough heat into the room to chase away the chill — well, from everywhere except her heart.

She had a problem on her hands, a big one that wasn't going to resolve itself. Something she couldn't fix from the cozy small town of Cedar Falls, Texas. There was no way around it; she was going to have to return to Louisiana. Soon. She wasn't sure why she'd lingered so long at her new sister-in-law's home.

Yes, I do. There was no point in lying to herself. The stately old mansion was so much more than a home. Her sister-in-law, Rachel, had transformed it into the Cedar Falls Finishing School for Young Ladies — a center of art, culture, beauty, and inspiration.

It was exactly the kind of place that Charity would've chosen to send her four-year-old daughter, if only it were in her price range. Unfortunately, her entire annual income as a seamstress wouldn't cover more than a few weeks at this place.

She rested her embroidery hoop on her knees as she cast a longing glance out of the tall, ornate window overlooking Harrington Gardens. On the west side of the gardens stood a new glassed-in greenhouse, named after the physician who'd built it for his four stair-step daughters who currently attended the school.

Charity huffed out a sad chuckle, unable to even fathom that kind of wealth. She couldn't afford the tuition, much less a corner of the grounds dedicated to her only daughter. No, indeed. There would be no Lucy Powers' flowerbed, potting shed, or even a closet constructed anytime soon for her namesake.

The more she thought about it, the more Charity wasn't sure why she and her daughter were even still here. They'd already long since outstayed their welcome, having lingered in Rachel's mansion a full month after her marriage to Boone.

My big brother. The thought of the tall and handsome former bounty hunter never failed to bring a smile to her lips. Some might claim he'd married up, but Charity knew better. He'd married just right. Despite Boone's gun slinging ways, he'd always been a patron of the arts. The man could dance and sing like an angel. He could play the harpsichord like one, too, plus spout poetry and smooth-talk a person into doing anything he wanted. No doubt those skills had come in handy during his career as a bounty hunter.

She shivered at the memory of the brute he'd joined forces with. Schmidt Barnes had served as his bounty hunting partner for the past seven years or so — an even taller, broader, hulking beast of a man. His longish, wind-blown blond hair did nothing to tame his menacing appearance. Anytime they were in the same room together, she might as well have been in the presence of Thor, the mythological god of war.

Instead of a hammer, he carried pistols, but he was every bit as deadly. Boone and Schmidt had made a name for themselves from coast to coast, hunting down and bagging their prey to collect the biggest bounties on the market. Their services were sought out by folks on both sides of the law. They'd even assisted a few federal marshals in handling border crimes — definitely not the kind of men others wanted to mess with.

Because of Boone's association with Schmidt, he was probably the richest black man in America right now. Even so, Charity was glad they'd finally parted ways. What Schmidt did for a living was too dangerous. Boone was far more suited to playing watchdog over the lovely young students attending the Cedar Falls Finishing School for Young Ladies. He'd already protected them from the first scoundrel who'd come their way. The next scoundrel would think twice about locking horns with a man of his sharp-shooting skills. Yes, indeed. The school was a much safer place with him around.

Charity couldn't have been happier that he'd stumbled across a vocation worthy of his well-tailored suits and debonair manner. She'd never seen him more content.

Charity let out a slow, long-suffering sigh, knowing it was going to be difficult to leave him behind and head back to Louisiana.

Oh, who am I trying to fool? She gripped her embroidery hoop so hard between her hands that she pricked a fingertip with her needle. With a whimper of pain, she popped the injured appendage into her mouth to keep from dripping blood on the white linen cloth she was decorating.

If she was being perfectly honest with herself, the only reason she hadn't yet departed for home was because she was in no hurry to leave such luxuries behind. Every minute of watching Lucy study and learn at the Cedar Falls School for Young Ladies had been like watching the miracle of a fresh rosebud unfurl in the sun.

Lucy pranced around the mansion and gardens like a little princess. Quite simply, the place suited her. Like her Uncle Boone, she'd always had a penchant for finer things. She adored dancing, singing, and twirling through life in ruffled dresses.

She was even learning how to play the grand piano in the parlor, beneath the auspices of Headmistress Rachel Cassidy. It was almost comical seeing the tiny dark fairy of a child perched on such a high bench, plinking one and two fingers at a time through classical old songs that everyone could recognize. She hadn't yet mastered the art of reading music, so most of what she played was by ear.

Rachel had assured Charity over and over again that it meant Lucy had a real ear for music, just like Boone. It made Charity feel all the more guilty about how soon she would be taking her daughter away from it all — from the long line of paintings in the gallery to the hundreds of leather-bound volumes lining the bookcases in the library.

But they couldn't stay here forever. *More's the pity!*

Every room had a theme, a purpose, and a name. Charity and Lucy happened to be staying in the Parisian suite. Still sucking on her finger, she stood and moved to the washbasin to rinse off her hand. She kept her fingertip beneath the water until the trickle of red stopped oozing.

Then she wrapped it in a scrap of white linen from her sewing basket and tucked the end in place.

There!

While she waited for the throbbing to subside, she strolled in a slow circle around the spacious room to soak in the sheer loveliness of it. The walls were papered in wide, pale pink and gilded gold stripes. An oversized four-poster bed anchored the space, with white lace curtains drawn back and held in place by tiny parakeet filigrees. Charity wondered if the whimsical little birds were fashioned out of real gold, though she was too proud to ask.

An enormous silk area rug was held in place by the foot-board, eliciting a sigh of appreciation from her. Even the rugs in her brother and sister-in-law's home were works of art! This one was woven in an intricate design of French vineyards with brightly dressed children playing a game of tag among countless rows of ripened grapes.

"It's fit for a queen," she murmured, as she spun in a circle to admire the rest of the furnishings for the umpteenth time. There was a vanity table with a stool, a writing desk, two antique wardrobes, and an honest-to-goodness fireplace with real flames licking at a pile of hickory logs. There was no huddling around a solitary wood stove in the kitchen for Rachel Cassidy's students. Nearly every room in the mansion possessed its own source of heat.

"What are you mumbling about now, child?" The elder Mrs. Cassidy's voice made Charity jump.

"Oh!" She whirled to face her mother, making her long calico gown swirl around her ankles. It was her newest creation — a collection of rose-red blooms and leaves on a bleached-white fabric. Wearing samples of her own work had turned out to be the best form of advertisement for her services. Other women often stopped her to ask who her seamstress was.

"Good morning, Mama." Charity wondered what she wanted. Her mother rarely did anything without an agenda, not even greet her own daughter. "I didn't hear you come in."

"I didn't knock." Mrs. Cassidy's delighted cackle seemed to warm the room another few degrees. She moved farther into the room, her ivory handled cane thumping with each step. "There's a matter of importance I wanted to discuss with you." She carefully lowered her ample curves onto the window seat Charity had vacated, careful to avoid the needle her daughter had stuck so carelessly into her hoop.

Now what?

"Here, Mama. Let me get that out of your way." Charity hurriedly crossed the room to return her embroidery project to her sewing basket on the floor beside the bench. As her hands moved, her mind flew busily. Perhaps, her mother was coming to remind her in no uncertain terms just how thoroughly she and Lucy had outstayed their welcome here.

"You and all your fancy seamstress work." Mrs. Cassidy sniffed in derision. "What is it now, child? Yet another fancy collar or skirt for that granddaughter of mine? You're going to spoil her rotten if you keep it up. You know you will."

Charity stared at her for a moment, not having expected to be the butt of such sharp criticism. "Sewing is my liveli-hood, Mama." It was difficult to control her voice with the way she was seething on the inside. *It's the way I keep food on the table for us all, remember? Back home, where the cook doesn't magically appear with a feast in hand every time you ring a silly bell!*

No matter how much she fumed inside her head, though, she never sassed back when her mother was in one of her lecturing moods. It didn't matter how much she might disagree. After a strict upbringing, she was convinced the outspoken and opinionated woman was still capable of taking a switch to her, despite her own twenty-two years. It was a theory she did not plan to test.

"You spoil her mercilessly!" Mrs. Cassidy peered at her daughter through her spectacles. They made the look she was giving her appear all the more severe.

"I reckon I learned from the best, ma'am," Charity returned cheerfully, well aware that her mother was forever sneaking cookies to her only grandchild. "How are your feet feeling this morning?"

"Fair to middling," her mama grumbled, which probably meant her gout was plaguing her something awful.

"How about some tea?" She glided to the sideboard to lift the pink porcelain teapot that the cook delivered to her room every morning. She filled teacups for the two of them, breathing in the soothing scent of peppermint that wafted up from the steaming spout.

Oh, how I'm going to miss this!

Her mother sniffed the air suspiciously. "That smells like one of Pansy's special recipes. Please assure me you didn't trouble her to make it for you when you've got two good arms and legs of your own."

Pansy was the Cassidys' dumpling of a cook — as short, round, red-cheeked, and animated as a fairytale creature. That is, until she opened her mouth and set the world straight about her true origins with her starchy British accent.

"No, ma'am. I wouldn't think of troubling Pansy for anything," Charity murmured, biting back a smile as she delivered one of the teacups to her mother. Yes, Pansy had prepared the tea, but it was something she insisted on doing. She'd chased Charity out of the kitchen on more than one occasion when she'd offered to help. The woman was tickled to death to have found such a willing taste tester in one of her guests. She tried a new and different flavor out on Charity nearly every single morning.

"Thank you, dear." Her mother accepted it gratefully. "I've got a hankering for it this morning like you wouldn't believe."

It was all the more proof that her gout was acting up again. She nearly always tried to drown her pain in tea.

"Drink all you want, Mama. It's a full pot." Charity lifted her own teacup for a delicate sip, enjoying the swirl of tantalizing steam.

"Join me." Mrs. Cassidy propped her cane against the wall and patted the cushion next to her. "I've been hoping to catch you alone to ask about the telegram you received yesterday."

Charity's insides grew cold, despite the tea they were sipping. She gave what she hoped was a careful wave of dismissal. "It was nothing important. Why do you ask? Is Boone being nosy again?" She forced a teasing note into her voice, recalling that her brother had been in the music room at the time of its delivery. Though participating in a dance lesson, he'd pivoted her way long enough for his dark gaze to narrow on the hand she was gripping the telegram with. She'd have to be more careful around him in the future. He was all too adept at picking up on the smallest details like that. Yes, she was worried about the contents of the telegram, but she was a grown woman now. She could take care of her own problems.

Mrs. Cassidy fixed her with one of her most owl-like

mama stares. "How I found out about the telegram is of no consequence. I have a right to worry about my own daughter if I've a mind to." Her eyes snapped with brown fire. "Which I am, so out with it! What has your pretty face in such a wretched pucker?"

"It's nothing, Mama. Really." Sickness curdled in her midsection at the thought of her mother getting involved in something so sordid. She'd been hoping the whole messy affair would die a natural death after she'd been gone a full month from Louisiana.

"So help me, Charity Belle Powers," her mother growled in a voice that indicated she wouldn't be taking no for an answer.

"If you insist on knowing, ma'am," Charity sighed, fearing she was opening a can of worms. "It's just some highfalutin' solicitor from Lafayette claiming my dearly departed husband owed him for a gambling debt."

"What?" Her mother nearly dropped her teacup. "Since when?"

"Since never! The man is sorely mistaken, and I'm about to write him back and tell him so." *For the third time!* Charity couldn't believe her mother would even suggest otherwise. "Jacob was no gambler. I know for a fact that he always brought his paychecks home. Every single penny." It had been three full years since Jacob Powers' passing, for crying out loud! It was disheartening that any scoundrel would raise his head after all this time, in an attempt to sully the name and reputation of a dead man.

"How much?" Mrs. Cassidy asked sharply.

Charity was so awash with memories that all she could do was blink at the question.

"How much money is the man asking for, child?" her mother elaborated impatiently. The worried creases at the corners of her eyes told Charity that she'd indeed opened a can of worms by answering her mother's questions. The woman wasn't even close to letting the matter go.

"Thirty-eight dollars and seventy-five cents," she supplied wearily. *Please let it go, Mama.*

"Is that all?" Her mother's voice was crisp with suspicion.

"For now. He claims that's the interest that's been building for the past few years. It'll take another two hundred to pay off the rest." Charity was unable to suppress the shiver that vibrated its way through her shoulder blades.

"I see." Her mother reached for her cane and used it to haul herself heavily to her feet.

"Whoa there, Mama!" Charity lunged for the teacup sloshing precariously in her other hand. "There's no need to get all worked up over nothing. As I've already stated, the man is sorely mistaken. We'll get to the bottom of this misunderstanding soon enough." Or so she prayed. "It's not like he's going to march right up to the front door and try to collect the funds himself. Lafayette is over four hundred miles away."

"Is that so?" Mrs. Cassidy snapped. "He already found out what town you're visiting and where you're staying, didn't he?"

Charity smiled bitterly. So much for trying to placate her mother with empty assurances. She was far too clever for that.

Her mother thumped her cane with alacrity all the way to the open bedroom door before turning around. "Are you going to tell Boone yourself, or will I have to?"

Charity averted her face as she returned their teacups to the sideboard. "What makes you think I haven't already told him, Mama?" She hadn't, of course. He was a newlywed, enjoying his first taste of marital bliss. If it weren't for the opening of the new finishing school, he and Rachel would be on their honeymoon.

"Well, now. Let me think." Her mother dramatically tapped one finger against her dark chin. "Maybe it has something to do with the seamstress work you agreed to do for Rachel and her students yesterday evening. For pay," she added slyly. "We both know you've been sewing pretty little things right and left for the girls the whole time you've been staying here. Why accept money for your services now, all of a sudden?" She lowered her hand to her side and continued in an accusing tone. "No. Not only have you *not* told your brother, you've decided to pay off that scoundrel, haven't you?"

"And what if I have, Mama?" In an uncharacteristic display of spirit, Charity rounded on her mother, slapping her hands to her slender hips. "It's my problem, and you can rest assured I'm going to handle it for all our sakes." Especially Lucy's. One did not simply dither around with a loan shark. It was too risky. If the man could not be convinced he'd contacted her by mistake, then she'd have no choice but to pay him.

Her mother thumped her cane again. "If you're so dead set on paying a debt you're not convinced is even yours, why not let Boone advance you the money? It would be better to owe your family than an outsider."

Charity spared her a tight smile. "I'm handling it, Mama. I truly am." She hurried across the room to step between her and the door. "So before you take things into your own hands and create a stew over something I'm already fixing, let me remind you of something. Boone just got married. He doesn't need his poor relations raining their shabby little burdens down on his wonderful new life. Let him be happy, Mama. For just a little longer, at least."

Her mother didn't look the least bit pacified. "How long is a little longer, child?"

"I don't know. A few weeks, maybe?" Charity had no idea if their interfering mother was capable of lasting that long without spilling the beans. Perhaps, by some miracle, she'd have the debt paid off by then and her late husband's name cleared.

Her mother made a pfft sound and stormed out the door.

Eight hours later

"Hand it over, Charity," Boone snarled. He stalked across the long library and came to stand directly in front of her.

Though her heart sank at his tone, she feigned a look of innocence from her perch on a backless sofa. It was upholstered in a rich tapestry of tropical trees and ridiculously cheery macaws that probably cost more than her entire cottage back home.

"Now!"

She'd never seen him this angry, and it was a tad unsettling. The way he stopped to tower over her was even more unsettling. Never before had his steely strength and iron-clad determination been so pointedly directed at her. In that moment, she could easily understand how he'd been so successful as a bounty hunter.

His darkly handsome features were twisted with fury. Though clad in one of his signature black silk suits and snowy white shirts with the silver cufflinks he adored so much, his gentlemanly demeanor was long gone. He looked ready to wrestle a wildcat.

She playfully swatted at the large hand he had extended in her direction, palm up.

His hand didn't budge.

Swallowing a sigh, she dug in her pocket and pulled out the crumpled telegram. "I don't know why everyone is making such a tempest in a teapot about it," she grumbled, slapping it into his hand. "I know Mama means well, but she had no business bending your ear over something I asked her to keep quiet about."

Not bothering to respond, Boone smoothed open the slip of paper and held it higher. He adjusted the angle of it a few times to catch the light from the crystal chandelier overhead. At least three dozen candles flickered from it, a nearly unheard of extravagance. Back home, Charity would have economized and stretched out those thirty-six candles for weeks.

"I say this bears looking into." His expression was grim, his voice flat.

Charity's gut wrenched in dismay. She knew what "looking into" something meant in Boone's world. It was his way of saying he planned to get involved and do a little of his own investigating. "But you're retired," she protested.

"Protecting my sister is as good a reason as any to come out of retirement." He neatly folded the telegram. Instead of handing it back, however, he tucked it inside the pocket of his dinner jacket.

"And married!" she reminded, hopping to her feet. "Rachel needs you here, and the students need you as well." She was so agitated, she hardly noticed how loud she was getting or how vehemently her hands were flapping.

"Did I hear my name?" Rachel Cassidy glided into the

room in a queenly gown of rose velvet. She glanced curiously between the two of them, tucking a stray dark curl behind one ear. "Please assure me I'm not interrupting anything. I can make myself scarce if I need to."

For an answer, Boone held out his arms to her.

Charity watched the way the harsh lines in his face softened like butter as his wife sailed into his embrace. She stood on her tiptoes to brush her lips against his jaw. A mixture of adoration and helpless longing infused his expression as his gaze met his wife's. They exchanged a look more intimate than a dozen kisses.

Suspecting the two of them had all but forgotten her presence, Charity took a cautious step towards the wide, arched doorway. Though it was January, Rachel still had every nook and cranny of the mansion draped with pine boughs and holly berries. The arched doorway had a particularly lovely one woven with red ribbons. Charity tried to tiptoe past it as quiet as a mouse, hoping to slip from the room unnoticed.

"Not so fast, my dear sister." Boone's voice made her freeze before she'd taken more than two steps.

Land sakes! It was as if the entire world was plotting to bring her down today. Charity drew a deep breath and spun back in his direction, forcing a smile to her lips. "Yes?" Upstairs in the Parisian room, she had no less than three dresses waiting to sew and seven collars to embroider, and not one of them was going to stitch themselves.

"You are right about how much I'm needed at home right now, sis." There was no denying the love etched deeply into his features as he continued to caress his wife with his eyes. There was also no denying the concern when he finally wrenched his gaze away from her and returned his attention to his sister. "Which leaves only one other option I can live with. If there ever was a job made for Schmidt Barnes, this one has his name painted all over it."

"I agree wholeheartedly." Unashamed of the fact Charity was still watching them, Rachel smoothed her hands over the lapels of his suit jacket. Then she busied herself straightening his tie, clearly in no hurry to quit fluttering like a butterfly over him. "Not to mention a visit to the school might make him take your retirement a bit more seriously."

Boone snorted. "I don't think anyone takes my retirement all that seriously. The sheriff keeps telling me there's a badge with my name on it when I'm ready to join his posse of deputies."

The rest of what he said faded into the background as Charity fumed over his earlier statement.

Send for Schmidt Barnes? Ugh! She tipped her head to the ceiling, not bothering to muffle her groan this time. The last thing she needed was another man blustering over her. It really wasn't fair of her brother to snap his fingers and drag in reinforcements like that. He was already bigger than her, stronger than her, and did enough fussing and fuming to equal a small army.

It really, really, really didn't help that her memories of her few, brief encounters with his former business partner were a jumble of tousled blonde locks too long to be considered fashionable, piercing blue eyes that saw more than a person wanted him to see, and square-jawed stubbornness.

I'm truly doomed. If Boone and Schmidt joined forces to interfere in her affairs, she could probably kiss her independence, privacy, and peace of mind goodbye for the foreseeable future.

"Men!" she hissed to no one in particular and fled the library.

Chapter 2: Rapid Fire Visit

Schmidt Barnes settled back in one of the plush, upholstered chairs in his private train car. It was going to be a long ride from Louisiana to Texas, the better part of three days with stops. He was ever a man on the move and tended to travel as lightly as possible — usually with no more than a single travel bag in hand — but that didn't mean he couldn't do it in both comfort and style.

The truth was, he could afford to travel any way he wanted these days. He had money deposited in banks from New York to California. And since he didn't maintain a permanent address or own any sizable trappings, such as furniture, the interest in his bank accounts continued to pile up. Someday, he would use the money to settle down on a piece of land of his own. A man like him would require a few hundred acres. Plenty of room to hunt and roam. Plenty of room to breathe.

He reached up with two fingers to loosen the collar of his dress shirt. A few days on a train didn't leave a man nearly enough room to breathe. However, Boone Cassidy's telegram was scorching the inside pocket of his jacket. He'd included their pre-agreed-upon signal of distress. One simple word. *Now*. It was short and to the point, a word that didn't cost much to include in a telegram and wouldn't arouse the suspicions of anyone transmitting the message from one part of the country to another. It meant Boone needed his help. Don't ask questions. Don't delay. Just come.

He wondered if it had anything to do with the ten thousand dollar bounty some hoodlum had just finished putting out on the man's sister. *Good gravy!* He was pretty sure that Charity Belle Powers could be bought and sold a dozen times over for that amount of money. It had to be a mistake.

He'd wasted no time hightailing it to Lafayette to make it clear that he intended to be the one to collect the bounty. His name alone should scare a few of the smaller thugs out of the game. Thankfully, Charity hadn't been in town. Neither had her mother. He could only hope it meant they were both safe in Texas with Boone.

The fellow he'd met with in Lafayette had insisted on meeting at a remote inn on the outskirts of town — outside under the cover of darkness, which in no way explained the expensive cut of his suit or the ring glinting from his pinky finger. Nor had the fellow been willing to give him a straight answer as to what Charity had done to deserve a bounty that size on her head. He'd mumbled something vague about her and her late husband being thieves, but he hadn't made eye contact while making the claim. When pressed, he couldn't even verify the accuracy of the claim.

Schmidt's mind had immediately jumped to other possibilities — that someone had issued a revenge hit of some sort on his former business partner, and they were merely using his sister as a means to get to him.

What in the world have you gotten yourself into this

time, my friend? Unable to remain seated, Schmidt pushed to his feet and paced the length of the car. Boone was supposed to be a happily married man, retired from bounty hunting and living the American dream. Schmidt sorely regretted not being able to attend his and Rachel's wedding. Such were the trials of bounty hunting. He had to go wherever the job led, and the last assignment he'd accepted had taken him all the way to California. On the upside, it meant one more man with a price on his head was now behind bars. *Good riddance!* He had little patience for folks who didn't respect the law and the rights of others.

That was something he and Boone had always seen eye-to-eye on. It was why they'd always worked so well together. Blowing out a breath, he reached up to scrub a hand over the scruff on his jaw. If he was being honest with himself, Boone was about the only man on earth he cared to work with. The only other fellow he'd tried taking on as a partner in recent months had tried his patience to the bone. He hadn't come close to measuring up to Boone's work ethic. His friend was ruthless yet fair, fearless yet brave, with just the right amount of caution thrown in. He could additionally think on his feet and keep a cool head while under pressure.

In short, he was irreplaceable. The rest of Schmidt's career stretched before him, a lot lonelier and duller than it had been with Boone by his side.

He stooped to peer through one of the narrow train windows, propping his hands on the custom wood panels above it. Miles of desert sand stretched beyond the glass, punctuated by cacti and Joshua trees. After a few moments, he fisted his hands and thumped them against the wall. He couldn't stand the thought of losing his partner permanently to retirement. There just had to be a way to get Boone back. Perhaps answering his friend's summons would open the door to that conversation. Sure, the man had every right to enjoy his new marriage for the time being. If anyone deserved to find a bit of happiness in this world, Boone was that man. He'd lost his first wife in childbirth and had waited a long time for his second chance at love.

But Schmidt knew Boone well enough to know he wouldn't be able to survive forever on the sweet regard of any woman, no matter how much in love he might be at the moment. Eventually, he would need a real job to sink his teeth into again. The thrill of a mission. The challenge of bringing bad hombres to justice. Like Schmidt, he thrived on helping those less fortunate than themselves, on righting the wrongs in this world one bounty hunting assignment at a time. There was no way he'd give up that feeling forever. It simply wasn't in his makeup.

It was entirely possible that the bounty on his sister's head would be all it would take to pull him back into the game.

Schmidt was almost disappointed when no highwaymen attempted to hold up his train at gunpoint. He wouldn't have minded seeing a little more action during the long trip west. Unfortunately, there wasn't the least sign of trouble the entire journey. He was downright twitchy with boredom by the time he arrived at the Cedar Falls Train Depot.

He irritably adjusted his silver bolo in the mirror over the washbasin, yanked a brown leather vest over his white dress shirt, and jammed a well-worn Stetson on his head. After a few seconds of contemplation, he unbuttoned his cuffs and rolled up his sleeves.

Much better. Those nasty cuffs are way too confining. He curled his upper lip at his reflection in the mirror. Probably could use a haircut, too, but Boone was accustomed to his shaggy appearance, and there was no woman in his life to impress. His choice of careers hadn't left any time for that.

Turning away from the mirror, he snatched up his travel bag and swaggered off the train. At least he'd gotten some decent rest on the bed in the back of the car. It was way too bad he couldn't bottle up some of it and save it for the next big job. Many of his assignments required overnight vigils.

Rolling his shoulders to loosen the stiffness of inactivity from them, he stepped onto the wide platform and surveyed his surroundings. So this was the cozy little Texas town that had wooed his business partner away from bounty hunting.

Cedar Falls certainly wasn't one of the biggest cities he'd passed through. However, he immediately recognized the appeal it might hold for a man like Boone. For one thing, it possessed a giant dose of small-town charm — from the newly constructed post office and bookstore on his left to the cafe and bank on his right.

The streets were bustling with activity. A number of wagons and carriages were rolling by on the road directly in front of him. A handful of cowboys were clopping slowly down the street on their horses, and all sorts of other folks were strolling around in high cotton in their brightly colored coats, hats, gowns, and suits. The town and the people in it were as pretty as a painting on the wall.

He let out a low whistle as a sleek black carriage wove its way around the other carriages and nosed its way directly in front of the platform. Its driver was wearing a smart black-and-white uniform and an attitude that suggested his employer owned half the town. The tall black man seated beside him could certainly afford to buy as much of the town as he wanted to.

Well, if that doesn't beat all! Schmidt shook his head in bemusement as Boone Cassidy leaped down to the ground in a fancy pinstriped suit and top hat. He continued to stare, openmouthed, as his former business partner proceeded to walk around the carriage and open the door with a princely flourish.

One of the loveliest women he'd ever had the pleasure of laying eyes on laid her hands on Boone's shoulders and allowed him to lift her down from the carriage. Boone's wife, he presumed, from the adoring way she tipped her face up to his.

Boone trailed one dark finger down her porcelain cheek before settling his arm possessively around her shoulders. Then he turned with her to face the train platform. His proud smile immediately brightened another several degrees.

"Schmidt!" With a quick, apologetic glance down at his lovely bride, he left her side to bound up the stairs two at a time.

"You old grizzly bear, you!" Boone's grip would have crushed the hand of a lesser man. He leaned in to clap his longtime partner between the shoulder blades, then took a step back to survey him. "Haven't changed one bit." There was satisfaction in his voice and no small amount of relief.

"Can't say the same about you." Schmidt was none too pleased about his partner's request to retire from their bounty hunting business, and he hadn't bothered to hide the fact. "If you looked any happier, your face might crack."

Boone guffawed and swung a fist at his shoulder. "Then may my bride and I have many long years ahead of cracking together." Without waiting for a response, he beckoned Schmidt to follow him down the stairs.

"Darling, this is Schmidt Barnes. Schmidt, my lovely bride, Rachel." Pride and joy glowed in Boone's dark features and vibrated in his voice.

"We meet at last." Rachel's voice was soft and cultured. She held out both gloved hands to Schmidt.

Surprised to receive such an open-faced welcome from such an uppity creature, he dropped his travel bag with a thud. He awkwardly took her hands in his, unsure what the protocol was for shaking two hands at the same time.

She gave them a brief but firm squeeze, then let them go. "I've heard so much about you that I feel as if we already met." She bestowed a warm, beauteous smile on him that left him feeling a little dazed.

He didn't know if hearing much about him was a good thing or a bad thing. Stories about him and Boone working together ranged from silent, overnight vigils to full-blown shootouts. He arched an eyebrow at her and waited for any sign to indicate her true opinion on the matter.

She gave a musical laugh. "There's no need to look so alarmed, Mr. Barnes. Not all of his stories about you were completely horrid." The teasing note in her voice, however, underscored the fact that some of them were less than savory, indeed.

"Schmidt," he offered, utterly mesmerized by the laughing glint in her eyes. Not only was she beautiful, she possessed a solid sense of humor. He sensed he was in the presence of someone intelligent and clever. *Ah, my friend, I see what happened here.* He shot Boone a knowing look. *You never stood a chance, did you?* No man with red blood running through his veins could've resisted such loveliness.

Boone's wife nodded in demure acquiescence of his offer. "Please address me as Rachel. I know we've only just become acquainted, but Boone has always spoken of you like you're family. That makes you my family as well."

Family, eh? Unsure what to say to that, he merely nodded. Out of the corner of his eye, he saw Boone pick up his travel bag and toss it on top of the carriage. He supposed that Boone was the closest thing he had to family now that his mother was gone. She'd passed the previous year. So if Rachel wanted to welcome him into her inner web, he was willing to play along. For now. At least until he could find a way to extract Boone from beneath her spell.

Grinning at him, Boone held open the carriage door and nodded at Schmidt to climb inside.

Ignoring his friend's gesture, Schmidt first crooked his arm at Rachel, beckoning her to allow him to lift her inside first. With an amused glance in her husband's direction, she allowed Schmidt to do exactly that.

He climbed in after her and took a seat across from her, running his hands appreciatively over the burgundy velvet cushion. He propped his arms across the back of the seat on either side of him and stretched out his legs. *Ah.* A fellow could get used to this kind of luxury.

Instead of hopping back up beside the driver, Boone joined them in the carriage and claimed the seat beside his wife. "Speaking of family, my mother and sister are in town."

"And your niece," Rachel added softly.

"Are they well?" Schmidt abruptly dropped his arms from the back of the seat and leaned forward. His bounty hunter senses prickled at the tenor in his friend's voice. Was he about to find out why he'd been summoned to Texas?

"As far as their health goes, yes." Boone shot him a dark look that indicated he was indeed ready to talk business. In front of his wife, no less. "That said, I could use your help keeping an eye on them for a few days. My sister, in particular."

Schmidt knew without asking that his friend hadn't called him into town to play nursemaid, which meant whatever was troubling his family was bad. Very bad. "I made a beeline for the train station as soon as I read your telegram," he assured. After a quick detour to the sheriff's office to collect his final bounty payment, of course.

"I'm mighty grateful you did." Boone's dark brow was wrinkled with worry. "Call me an overprotective fool for taking such drastic measures, but my gut hasn't rested easy since I found out there's a fellow from the bayou hounding her for money."

Hounding *her* for money? Schmidt scowled in concentration at his friend, wondering why his friend hadn't started the conversation by mentioning the bounty on her head. However, Boone's gut was never wrong. If he was coming at the situation from another angle, Schmidt was all ears.

"Tell me everything," he demanded. Where family was involved, all boundaries and rules went out the window. The two of them would protect Boone's sister, no matter the reason and no matter the cost.

"The telegram came from somewhere on the outskirts of Lafayette. I'm not familiar with the name, but I suspect he's a loan shark from how he worded his message. One of the shadier ones, I'm guessing."

Is there any other kind of loan shark? Schmidt knew

without asking that Boone was referring to a gambling operation. There were all too many of them infesting the coastal cities these days. It was clear that he was trying to avoid alarming his wife with more details than necessary.

When he fell silent, Schmidt prodded, "Any idea how long she's been involved with the likes of him?" It sickened him to learn that his friend's pretty little sister had fallen prey to such a weakness. He'd watched the addiction destroy more lives than he cared to keep count of.

"What?" Boone's expression reminded Schmidt of a volcano ready to erupt. "You can't possibly think—?"

Schmidt slapped the air to cut off his tirade. "Well, what was I supposed to think? You're doling out details like a French chef handing out a tray of bite-sized petit fours. Out with it, man!"

Looking supremely annoyed, Boone growled, "He signed his name as Morley. Just Morley. No way of telling if it's a first name or a last name. He claims her late husband has an outstanding debt of a couple hundred dollars, which makes no sense. Jacob Powers was as clean as a whistle." Boone fisted his hands so tightly on his knees that the blood left his knuckles.

A debt, not a bounty. A couple hundred dollars versus the ten thousand I'm supposed to be trying to collect. The numbers sure weren't matching up. Schmidt nodded slowly as it dawned on him that his friend must not have heard about the bounty yet. *I reckon I'm about to make your day that much worse.*

And some creep named Morley was right in the middle of it all. Anger simmered through Schmidt's bones. "Didn't Mr. Powers pass away a few years ago?" If Schmidt's memory served, his death wasn't all that recent. That detail alone shed suspicion on the demand for money.

"Three years and change," his friend fumed. "After I contacted you, I did some digging around about this Morley. Fired a message off to a few of my mother's friends. So far, no one has seen hide or hair of anyone by that name around Lafayette."

Schmidt wasn't sure what to make of that. One thing was for sure. Morley was the sort of person who didn't mind terrorizing a vulnerable woman from the shadows. Why Charity Powers, though? She was a grieving widow, single mother, and poor as a church mouse. So unless she was quietly living a life of crime that no one in her family knew about, the crosshairs on her forehead made little sense. No wonder Boone was ten shades of worried about her.

Schmidt wasn't quite ready to tip his hand about the bounty. He still had a few questions first. "Let me guess," he drawled coolly. "Your sister is desperate to pay off the note. She wants to clear the good name of her beloved late husband." It was an age-old con, one the perpetrators didn't usually wait three years to pull. It was easier to extort money from someone wallowing in fresh grief.

Rachel leaned her slender form closer to meet Schmidt's gaze directly. She rested one delicate hand on her husband's forearm, as if trying to tamp down on his growing agitation. "Yes. That's exactly what's going on. We first suspected something was wrong when Charity came to me a couple of days ago asking for referrals for work. She's a seamstress. A highly skilled one, mind you. Even with her clever designs, though, it would take a long time for a woman of her humble means to pay off the amount he's demanding."

Boone made a groaning sound. "Actually, I knew some-thing was wrong the day she arrived in town. She's been

26

receiving way too many telegrams and all but hiding out in her room."

Rachel made a rueful face at him. "At first, we assumed she had an admirer from back home who misses her dearly, but her mama kept insisting that wasn't the case."

Boone grunted. "And you don't hide anything from Mama."

Schmidt decided that now was as good a time as any to lay his bad news on them. "I'll admit to being curious about something. What does your mama have to say about the bounty on your sister's head?"

For a moment, it grew so silent in the carriage that the only sound was the horses' hooves clopping against the hard-packed earth beneath them.

Boone's dark visage took on a slight red tinge. "What did you say?"

"Ten thousand dollars," Schmidt informed him coldly. It was a truly horrific sum, so horrific that it was hard to believe it was the first time Boone was hearing about it.

"For my sister," his friend said carefully. His expression was impossible to read.

Schmidt gave one hard up-down movement with his chin. "I boarded the next train for Lafayette to scare off as many low-level thugs as I could. Plus, I met with the contact listed on the bounty offer."

"And," Boone snarled.

"It was a dead end." Schmidt shook his head. "The fellow didn't know squat. He made some vague reference to your sister and her husband being thieves, but he backpedaled on the story pretty quickly when I asked for details. Said maybe he'd heard wrong. He doesn't know who's paying the bounty. Said he's working for a guy by the name of...you're not going to believe this." He watched

Boone and Rachel's faces closely as he said the name. "Morley.

They exchanged a long, worried look that told Schmidt none of what they were hearing was making any sense to them.

"We're going to get to the bottom of this, sweetheart," she whispered.

Schmidt studied the worry in her classical oval and cream features with new respect. Perhaps there was more to Boone's uppity headmistress of a wife than he'd originally presumed. She seemed to have a mighty brave head resting on her lovely shoulders. A lesser woman would've dissolved into tears after learning about the trouble dogging the heels of Boone's family. Instead, she was offering him comfort.

The carriage rolled up a short hill around a wide, circle cobblestone drive. Then it came to a stop.

All Schmidt could do was stare. Before him rose a castle of storybook proportions. It stretched on for what felt like miles of red and white stone. There were more arched windows than a body could shake a stick at and a pair of turrets. Turrets! They made his imagination conjure up things like medieval castles.

"Well, I'll be," he muttered, opening the carriage door and leaping down. He pivoted around to face his friends. "You live here? For real?"

Boone grunted as he assisted his wife to the ground. "Believe me, I felt the same way when I first laid eyes on the place."

Schmidt shook his head in amazement at the fortress rising in front of them. It might be harder than he originally presumed to pull his friend out of retirement. The man was living in the lap of kingly luxury.

A ball bounded in his direction. Without thinking, he

caught it with the toe of his boot and held it captive against the ground.

A high-pitched shriek of laughter filled his ears. Seconds later, a wiggling mass of girls with pink cheeks and flying arms emerged from behind a copse of naked oak trees. Braids, curls, coats, and boots of every color raced his way as each child sought to be the first one to reach the ball.

Schmidt watched in fascination as a tiny sprite of a child with burnished skin and coal-black braids burst ahead of their ranks and bounded like a jackrabbit in his direction. She reached him only a second or two ahead of the others. Gazing up at him beseechingly, she clasped her pink gloved hands against her chest. "Please, mister, may I have our ball back?"

Her resemblance to Boone was undeniable. An emotion completely foreign and wonderful wrenched Schmidt's insides. For a moment, he was convinced he was facing a fairy straight from the same storybook the castle beside them had risen from. The only thing she was missing was a set of gossamer wings. She was as coppery and sun-kissed as an exotic princess from some far-off land.

And then it hit him who she was. He was staring at Charity Powers' daughter. Boone's niece. She couldn't be more than four-years-old, maybe five, a tiny ray of inno-cence whose poor-as-dirt mother had a bounty on her head. Sometimes the world was a very unfair place.

Schmidt squatted down to bring himself eye-level with her as he handed over the ball. It killed him to realize she was going to need as much protecting as her mother in the coming days.

She blinked curious, almond-shaped eyes at him. Then she claimed the ball with a glorious smile. It blasted straight through his leather vest, straight to his heart, like a bolt of sunshine. He rocked back on his heels, utterly stunned, as she raced off with her friends. She was so full of life and energy, so unspoiled by a world that would be cruel to her in the coming years for nothing more than the breathtaking color of her perfectly unmarred skin.

The bounty on her mother's head was simply insult upon injury. His gut was screaming that they were innocent, both of them. They didn't deserve the trouble that had followed them from Lafayette. Something far more sinister must be going on, something that he intended to get to the bottom of.

He watched the girl's animated retreat, a bundle of tiny knees and elbows, and knew with sudden certainty there was nothing he wouldn't do to protect her and her mother — absolutely nothing. Boone was a loyal friend who'd saved his carcass more than once. Schmidt owed him no less than to help his sister out of whatever mess she'd gotten herself entangled in. He'd move heaven and earth if that was what it took. He'd lasso the moon and bring it crashing to the ground. He'd kick the infernal Morley so far into kingdom come for preying on such a precious child and her mother that...

Boone's hand came down on his shoulder. "That niece of mine is something else, isn't she?" Pride infused his voice. It was tinged with awe.

"She's incredible." Schmidt slowly rose to his feet. "She's..." He searched for the right words to describe such vibrance and life, but they evaded him. "What's her name?"

"Lucy."

Lucy Powers. Small yet mighty. Despite the dark cloud hanging over the child and her mother, Schmidt grinned at how well the name suited her.

The bright blue ball came careening in his direction

again. This time, he was prepared for it. He gave in to the youthful impulse to kick it back to Lucy.

Lucy giggled in delight. "Look," she shouted to the others, pointing merrily at him. "The big man is on my team."

Her team. *You bet your boots I am, princess!* With a rueful glance over his shoulder at Boone and Rachel, he joined in the game.

Chapter 3: Unexpected Roots

Arms folded in suspicion, Charity stood at the front parlor window, watching the tall hulk of a man kicking a ball around the front lawn with over half the students of the Cedar Falls Finishing School for Young Ladies. They were laughing hysterically at his antics as he pretended to be injured from how hard her daughter kicked the ball to him. The next time Lucy passed the ball to him, it went wide. He did a backwards somersault to reach it.

He was athletic. She'd give him that. He was also showing off, maddeningly so. The man was everything she remembered — too good looking and too cocky for his own good.

She heard the familiar tread of her brother's boots as he entered the adjoining foyer.

"This is your big plan for sorting out my affairs, eh?" She swiveled to face him as he set a black travel bag down by the stairs. It was plain and masculine, and there was only one bag. Clearly, Schmidt Barnes traveled light.

"I'd trust him with my life." Boone strolled into the

room, thumbs dangling from his belt loops. "And have on more than one occasion."

She waved a hand in agitation at the window. "He's nothing more than an overgrown child." It was hard to believe such a monstrous-sized creature was voluntarily horsing around the yard with a pack of rowdy children.

"Oh, he's a lot more than that, sister dear." He moved to stand beside her. Leaning her way, he kissed the top of her head.

Despite her irritation at him, her heart warmed at the gesture.

"Lucy likes him," he noted in a low voice. "Children don't fake that sort of thing." They were too young. Too innocent.

They stood together at the window. "I don't bring men around her, Boone." Charity shoved a handful of long, dark hair over her shoulder. "Not ever. She might get attached, and then what?"

"Every child needs a good male role model," he retorted. "I don't see any harm in her enjoying her time with her uncles."

"Uncles!" She rounded on him. "You're the only uncle she's got!" How dare he insinuate that overstuffed buffoon outside the window was in any way related to them!

"He's family," Boone interrupted sharply. "Like a brother to me, which makes him her uncle. Or as good as one."

With a sniff of disdain, she returned her attention to the game of ball taking place outdoors. She'd made it pretty clear that she preferred to handle her own problems, so there was no way she was accepting an outsider into her inner circle. She didn't care how close of a friend the wild grizzly bear of a man was to her brother. She was never going to consider Schmidt Barnes to be her family. He was too big, too rough around the edges. Not to mention he was the wrong color. Little black girls didn't possess giant white uncles, and that was that!

Boone's heavy arm encircled her shoulders. "We need him right now, Charity. You and Lucy, both."

She gave a gusty sigh of frustration. "I know you mean well, Boone. You truly do, and I love you for it. But please recall I never asked for your help in the first place. I'll be getting us out of your hair before long, and I'll be paying my own debts. No ifs, ands, or buts about it."

Boone's arm tightened around her. "About your visit, sis. Rachel and I believe with all our hearts that it would be best if you remain with us until we resolve this nasty bit of loan shark business."

She twisted in his arms to stare up at him in horror. "I most certainly will not! How can you even suggest such a thing? I may be your poor relation, but I refuse to burden you indefinitely with my presence. I already have a plan to pay off the note. I wish you and Mama would just leave it at that. Please?" Despite her bravado, her voice cracked a little. She hadn't been sleeping well lately. The stress of returning home to face her late husband's debts, mistaken or not, was wearing her nerves to a ribbon.

"You are *not* a poor relation!" He looked incensed at her words. "How dare you call yourself that!" He clenched his jaw. "I can well afford to make things easier on you and Mama. I don't see why you're being so stubborn about letting me."

"I *am* a poor relation, whether you like it or not," she snapped, "but I still won't be accepting any handouts. Not from you or anyone else!" She couldn't believe he was even suggesting it. "Take care of Mama all you want. She deserves to have things easier, but I'll be providing for my daughter and me." The mere thought of returning to Louisiana without Mama made her heart ache, but she would do it if she had to. Mama wasn't getting any younger, and she liked it here in Cedar Falls.

"Fine! Thumb your nose at my offer to help out with your debts all you want, but you won't be turning down my protection," he growled.

They glowered at each other, nose-to-nose. "Your safety is not up for negotiation," he continued. "You are my only sister, and Lucy is my only niece. Over my dead body will I allow anything bad to happen to either of you."

"Nor will I." The low male drawl had them both spinning around.

Charity stared at the newcomer in the parlor, taking in his windblown hair and cheeks reddened from the crisp winter breeze. Up close, Schmidt Barnes was even bigger, dustier, and more rugged than she remembered.

"Mr. Barnes," she intoned coolly. "It's been a coon's age." At least three years. She vaguely recalled his hulking presence in the rear of the church building at her husband's funeral. Unless her memory failed her, she hadn't laid eyes on him since.

"Too long," he agreed, clearly misunderstanding her words. He strode across the room to take one of her hands between his two much larger paws. He wasn't wearing gloves, so his cool, callused fingers brushed lazily over hers. "Figured it was past time to rectify such a gross oversight."

She shivered at his touch, and not just from his chilled fingers. He didn't seem in much of a hurry to let her hand go, which she found a tad flattering and even a tad more unnerving. She withdrew her hand, peeking shyly up at him from beneath her lashes.

He was surveying her with a troubled expression in his keen blue gaze, one that in no way masked the admiring glint in them.

Her insides twisted with confusion. Every instinct in her was screaming that his presence in her life was going to spell trouble. She could feel it all the way to her bones. However, she merely rolled her eyes at him. "Pfft! We both know the only reason you're in town is because my brother called in some sort of favor. A completely unnecessary gesture, I assure you." She tossed another scowl in Boone's direction. "Admittedly, I'm in a little financial trouble, but it's nothing I can't handle on my own, as I've stated to him again and again."

"Charity..." Boone's voice held a note of warning. "I apologize, Schmidt. I thought I made it clear that her safety is not negotiable."

"No offense taken," Schmidt assured, looking more amused than offended. "I've never been one for meaningless chitchat. I like a woman who's brave enough to lay her cards on the table. That way we can get down to business."

Brave? Charity's eyes widened at the unexpected compliment. Was he making fun of her? Brave wasn't exactly the adjective she would've used to describe herself. Discouraged, maybe, and a little afraid.

"Nonsense!" Rachel protested, breezing into the room with the soft swish of ivory and lavender velvet. "You've only just arrived. Please allow me to start your visit with a pot of tea. Sit." She fluttered her delicate hands at them. "All of you, I insist." She glided to the far side of the room and yanked on the gold chain dangling against the wall.

Instead of her cook, Mrs. Cassidy appeared. The thump of her cane warned them of her approach. She limped around the corner in her Sunday best navy wool dress.

"Schmidt!" Her round, dark face dissolved into joyous creases as a smile stretched across it. "Get over here, you big brute, and give your other mother some love."

Charity watched in astonishment as Schmidt obediently trotted across the room to enclose her feisty mama in a bear hug. Their embrace lasted much longer than she expected.

Other mother? Charity had no idea when they'd become such close friends. She hugged her arms around her middle, feeling wholly outnumbered and outmaneuvered as she slumped onto the corner of the sofa. Did it mean Mama was in on his sudden dash into town? The obvious affection between them made her feel like an outsider in the room, which only made her resent his presence all the more.

When Mrs. Cassidy finally disengaged herself from his embrace, her eyes were damp. "I'll let Pansy know you'll be needing tea and coffee." She brushed her fingertips across the corners of her eyes. "And a tray of my own made-from-scratch biscuits and preserves. Hopefully, that'll tide you over until dinner time."

Schmidt bent to deliver her another quick hug. "How can I say no to your biscuits? A man only has so much willpower." For some reason, he chose that moment to glance over his shoulder at Charity.

Their gazes clashed. *So much willpower, eh?* She scowled darkly at him. *I don't know how you wormed your way into her heart, mister, but you'll soon figure out I'm not such an easy mark.*

He grinned back unashamedly. His slow, lazy wink at her brought a wave of heat rolling up her neck. Unless she was mistaken, the brazen man was flirting with her, right beneath her strict mama's nose.

"Anything for you, son," Mrs. Cassidy purred. "It's the

least I can do for the way you've always looked after my Boone." Her expression clouded a trifle as her gaze drifted to Charity. "And the way you've rushed in to lend a hand with my sweet baby girl." A damp sigh escaped her. "She's my heart. She is. I couldn't bear for anything bad to happen to her."

Charity bit her lower lip, holding on to her fragile patience until her mother had thumped back down the hall towards the kitchen. Then she exploded on her brother. "How dare you worry Mama like that! What were you thinking, Boone?" She hated to upbraid him in front of his wife and friend, but he'd gone too far this time. Now that Mama knew Boone was concerned enough to call in additional help, the poor woman probably wouldn't sleep another wink until all of Jacob's debts were paid in full.

"It was...necessary." There was no mistaking the regret in Boone's voice.

She shook her head in exasperation at him. "For what?"

"To keep you in town for the time being, my dear."

What? "You didn't," she gasped, feeling faint. *You wouldn't stoop so low! You've always been on my side.* But one look at his face assured her he had, indeed, added their mother to his growing list of reinforcements against her. But he hadn't stopped there. He'd taken it a step further and convinced Mama that it wasn't safe for Charity to return home with Lucy.

"Why?" She spread her hands, trying to keep them from shaking. "I told you I'm handling Mr. Morley in my own way. You know I have plans to pay off my husband's debts once and for all." Her brother didn't have to like her methods, but the entire sordid situation would be behind them soon.

"You'll never pay him off," Schmidt announced in a flat

voice. "That's the trouble. Men like him will keep their hands outstretched. If you're foolish enough to hand over one blessed cent, he'll keep coming back for more."

"Foolish?" She glared indignantly across at him. "A few minutes ago, you said I was brave. Make up your mind!"

Instead of looking chastised, he smirked at her — actually *smirked!* "Perhaps you are both."

"He's right about this Morley creature." Boone nodded gravely, ignoring the testy little byplay taking place between his friend and sister. "What's worse, I can't dig up anything on the fellow. More than likely, that means he's operating under an assumed name. He's bad news, Charity."

She turned her glare in his direction. *I gathered that nugget of wisdom for myself. Thank you very much!* It still didn't explain why they were so convinced the man couldn't be paid off and sent on his way. She didn't want to spend the rest of her days with a debt hanging over her and Lucy's heads, not even a debt that had been sent their way by mistake. She'd rather pay it off and be done with it.

Schmidt didn't return to his seat. Instead, he came to tower over the end of the sofa where she was huddled. "Not only does he know where you and Lucy are staying right now, he likely knows where you live back in Lafayette, since that's where the bounty on your head originated from."

"The what?" The air left her lungs in a rush. For a moment, she swayed dizzily on the sofa cushion.

"Water! She needs water," Rachel cried somewhere in the distance.

Schmidt's concerned features went in and out of focus a few times as he crouched down in front of her. "There's a bounty on your head, Mrs. Powers. I take it you didn't know about it?"

She shook her head numbly, her eyes filling with tears.

"What's going on?" She choked out the words, feeling utterly deflated as her head swung weakly between him and her brother. If they were trying to scare her, it was working.

"I haven't figured that out yet. But when I do, you'll be the first to hear it, ma'am." There was a world of empathy in his voice that nearly proved to be her breaking point. He wasn't her enemy.

She wasn't sure why she'd been lashing out at him. "Charity," she rasped. "If you're truly here to help me escape heaven-only-knows-what, you might as well call me by my name, Mr. Barnes."

"Schmidt," he corrected harshly. "I boarded the first train to Lafayette after finding out about the price on your head."

She nodded, hearing his words but not really comprehending what they meant. *First, a debt I didn't know I had. Now, I have a bounty on my head? What next?* It felt like a bad dream, one she would surely wake from soon. She pinched her arm, just to be sure. Hard. "Ouch," she whispered.

A twinkle warmed Schmidt's icy blue gaze. "You haven't asked how much yet."

A sound that was half-laugher, half-sob escaped her. "I'm afraid to. Correction. I'm terrified to."

A glass of water was pressed into her hand. She was pretty sure Rachel had done it. "Thank you," she murmured to no one in particular.

"Take a drink first." Schmidt's voice was firm. "Then I'll tell you."

She forced herself to choke a sip past the lump in her throat. Then another.

"Ten thousand dollars," he announced quietly.

The glass slid from her grasp, or would have if he hadn't caught it.

He set it aside and took her hands in his. Her fingers had grown very cold, because his fingers felt impossibly warm against hers.

She shook her head at him and made a soft, bleating sound, but it was a long time before she could actually form any actual words. The room was spinning too fast around her. "I'm not worth that much." It must be a mistake. He'd heard wrong or read the announcement wrong or...

His hands tightened almost painfully on hers. "I beg to differ." His voice was so firm with conviction that the spinning sensation slowed. The room and its occupants and furnishings took their places once again. "I'm sure your family disagrees even more strongly with that statement."

Charity's lashes fluttered damply against her cheeks as she clung to his hands while seeking out her brother.

She found Boone leaning forward on the foot of the chaise lounge, where he was perched next to his wife. His forearms were resting on his knees, and his head was bowed over them as if the weight of the world was on his shoulders.

Rachel's hand crept along the underside of his arm, silently offering comfort. Without turning to look at her, Boone laced his fingers through hers. It was a wrenching moment for Charity. They had each other to share the load. It was a stark reminder that she had no one other than the slightly annoying behemoth of a man still crouching in front of her.

A man whose help she hadn't asked for. A man she barely knew. A man who thought she was both foolish and brave. A man who...

She blinked in astonishment at him. "You're here to haul me in and collect the bounty, aren't you?"

Rachel's gasp resounded across the room, and Boone's head came up, his jaw dropping in disbelief. "Charity," he groaned. "How many times have I told you...?" He shook his head, unable to finish the sentence.

Schmidt barked out a laugh and promptly straightened, letting go of her hands. Instead of saying anything, he took a seat beside her on the sofa.

She shot a wary look at her would-be bounty hunter and waited for someone to explain what was going on. When no one did, she spluttered, "Oh, give way! Surely, the thought has at least crossed your mind to turn me in and collect the money."

Schmidt shook his head. "No. Can't say that it has."

"Ten thousand dollars is a fortune," she protested.

He shrugged like it was no big deal. "There are more important things in life than money, Charity." He was so large that he took up more than his share of the sofa. The leg of his trousers brushed her skirt.

"Not to most people." She twitched her skirts away from him. Most of the folks she'd encountered between here and Lafayette would've been glad to trade a poor black woman for a sum far less than that.

"I'm not most people." His tone was deceptively mild, since she could practically feel the anger radiating off him. Strangely enough, his anger felt directed at her.

"Then I am glad you are not." Her voice shook a little. She was dangerously close to coming unraveled again. Too much had happened too soon. She'd yet to absorb it all.

Schmidt shifted restlessly beside her. For a moment, she thought he might take her hand in his again, but he didn't. "There could be any number of reasons why this Morley creature decided to target you," he mused in a low, tight voice. "I have a few theories and none of them good."

"Me, too." Boone studied his friend somberly. "They could be trying to get back at me, for instance. I've helped put plenty of bad hombres behind bars."

"Or they might have figured out your sister's true identity, and it's your mother he's really after. Or the nest egg your father left her, to be more precise." Schmidt's low, matter-of-fact voice droned through Charity, making her draw a quick breath. The irksome man had no business possessing such a delicious baritone that resonated straight through a person like that. "Think about it," he drawled in the same fiercely concerned voice. "Most mothers would hand over any amount of coin to make their daughters' problems go away, and Mrs. Cassidy is every bit the mother hen who would do such a thing. She thinks the sun rises and sets on Charity."

My true identity? Charity was half-tempted to pinch herself again. Nothing Schmidt was saying was making any sense to her. At the mention of her mother, however, she glanced around the room, wondering why it was taking Mama so long to return with her biscuits and jam. To her surprise, she found the tray of refreshments sitting on the coffee table. Apparently, Mama had already come and gone. Charity didn't blame her for not staying. Mama was probably in bed, having a fit of vapors over the bounty on her daughter's head. Poor woman! As if she didn't have enough to worry about already!

"Mama already offered to hand over her inheritance to Morley, and I already refused to let her," Boone confessed grimly. "You and I both know it won't do a bit of good. It might make matters worse, everything considered." He gave his friend a knowing nod.

"I d-don't understand." Charity recoiled at his cryptic declaration. "What inheritance?" The fact that Mama had money of her own was news to Charity. Since when? She'd always assumed it was Boone who was supporting their mother's humble existence back in Louisiana. She lived in a cozy cottage next door to Charity and Lucy on the bayou, cooked and baked for others to raise her grocery money, and owned exactly three dresses to her name — the one she worked in, the one she wore to church, and the somber black one she'd worn to Jacob's funeral.

Boone unlaced his fingers from Rachel's and moved across the room to crouch in front of his sister like Schmidt had done earlier. "I reckon it's time for you to know this." He drew a heavy breath. "My father passed away shortly after I was born."

She shook her head at him, not comprehending. "But that's impossible!" It would mean that Mr. Cassidy hadn't been her father, after all, since she was six years younger than Boone. And that would make Boone what? Her half-brother? She blinked rapidly at the horrifying thought. *No!* Mama wouldn't have kept something like that from her. How could she? And if the dearly departed Mr. Cassidy hadn't been her father, then who was?

"It's not impossible, sis. It's just not something Mama wanted to talk about."

"You mean I was born on the wrong side of the blanket?" Her voice cracked with humiliation.

"Not at all." He stared in irritation at her. "You have a habit of jumping to the worst conclusions possible!"

"A little grace," she pleaded. "I'm a woman with a bounty on my head," she reminded.

His mouth twisted wryly. "Mama remarried a few years after my father died. It was a hush-hush affair that few folks in town ever caught wind of. It's what Mama wanted, Charity. Things were different back then, you see."

Different! How? Feeling like she was about to be sucked beneath yet another muddy current, she pressed a hand to her bosom, forcing slow measured breaths into her lungs.

"No matter what I say next, you hang on to this, sis. Your father was a good man, you hear?"

She gulped and nodded, knowing that was his way of saying she wasn't going to like what he said next.

"His name was Charles Dunaway."

Her eyebrows shot upward. The only Dunaways she knew about were the ones who lived in the ritziest part of Lafayette. "Isn't that the mayor's name?"

He nodded gravely. "Yes. Rupert Dunaway is the son your father had by his first wife, may she rest in peace. The mayor is your half-brother, as am I."

"No!" The word tore out of her. *No.* She didn't want any uppity relations, certainly not ones as snooty as the Dunaways. She shook her head so vehemently that the tears she hadn't realized were forming started to spill down her cheeks. Though she had no personal memories of Boone's father, she adored all the stories her mother had told her about him over the years. No, it was more than that. She'd idolized the man in those stories. "Mr. Cassidy is the only man I've ever wanted for a father," she quavered. The pretty designs on the parlor wallpaper danced before her eyes. "The only one I'm claiming, at least."

Boone looked dismayed. "I regret you had to find out this way, but surely you've suspected something before now. It's why your skin is so much lighter than mine."

No. She shook her head at him again. She'd not once questioned it. There'd been no reason to. She'd merely accepted it as a natural phenomenon, which now seemed terribly naïve. Schmidt had been right to call her foolish.

She held out trembling hands to place them on top of

his much darker ones. Why did it suddenly feel like her wonderful big brother, whom she'd always depended on, was slowly slipping away from her? Like the closeness they'd always shared was somehow being dimmed.

"I didn't ask for this," she choked. "I don't want this. Any of it!" *I just want things to go back to the way things were when you first walked into the room. I want Mr. Cassidy to go back to being my father. I want you to go back to being my brother, my full blood brother.*

"Why, Charity!" He reached for her shoulders and shook them lightly. "This doesn't change a thing between us. You will always be my sister. Always and forever," he assured fervently.

Unable to face him or either of his fair-skinned "family members" in the room any longer, she wrenched herself from his grasp and fled to the entry foyer. She ran up the stairs, stumbling several times on her skirt.

Beyond the long, ornate railing, she perceived the shadowy figure of her mother hobbling in her direction with a tray in hand, but she couldn't face her right now, either. She desperately needed to be alone. She needed time to come to grips with the awful discovery that her straight-laced, God-fearing Mama had been lying to her about her roots her entire life.

It was almost too much to bear. Maybe Charity should've pinched herself harder earlier. Maybe then she would've proven she was merely wandering through a nightmare — one she desperately wanted to wake up from. Because if she didn't wake soon, there'd be no escaping the harsh truth.

My daddy was a white man!

Chapter 4: Protecting Lucy

To Schmidt's immense disappointment, the fiery-tempered Charity remained out of sight for the next several days.

"She'll come around," Boone assured him each time he inquired about her. "She's stronger than she looks. She just needs time to swallow everything we've told her."

Schmidt nodded, unable to blame the lovely widow for reeling a little beneath the weight of everything she was currently going through. It wasn't every day a person found out they had a bounty on their head...or that it might have something to do with a wealthy father they didn't know they had until now. A father Charity had never gotten to meet, for that matter, and never would get to meet. Schmidt could only imagine what a bitter pill it was for her to swallow.

His own upbringing wasn't anything to brag about. He'd been raised by a seasonal worker down south, who'd died when he was barely out of grammar school. He didn't know who his mother was. After his father's death, he'd continued to migrate from farm to farm with the other seasonal workers, pretending to be older than he was for the room, board, and meals that resulted from the lie. Sometimes his employers had paid him wages in addition to those other things. Sometimes they hadn't. On the upside, the back-breaking work had toughened him up. It was also how he'd met Boone and his mother. At the time, they'd been working for the man Mrs. Cassidy would later marry.

Mr. Dunaway had been one of the kindest, fairest task masters in the south. He was also the first man who'd paid Schmidt an adult wage. Schmidt had used it to purchase his first train ticket to hunt down his first bounty. A couple of years later, he'd returned south to invite Boone to become his partner, and the rest was history.

Schmidt couldn't wait to tell Charity his side of the story about meeting her father. Maybe finding out what a good man Mr. Dunaway had been would cheer her up a little. Despite her brother's insistence that she'd resurface when she was ready, and not a minute before, he found himself keeping a hawk-eye out for her. While he waited, he stayed busy with some good old-fashioned detective work about the loan shark situation. He also took some time to get to know Charity's spunky daughter better.

Instead of boarding at the Cedar Falls Inn like Schmidt expected, Rachel had extended an invitation for him to stay in the old carriage house with her gardener, Hodge Jenkins. At least that's what the man insisted on being called. Mr. Jenkins, as it turned out, was actually far more than a gardener. From what he could tell, the man was Rachel's right-hand man, second only to Boone. He puttered around the house and grounds in a black-and-white uniform that Boone insisted was more his idea than Rachel's, ensuring everything at the school remained in excellent repair. Nighttime was a different story, however. After the man's third nightly disappearance, Schmidt followed him and discovered him patrolling the estate with a hunting rifle resting against his shoulder.

"Good evening, sir," he called jovially, not wanting to startle the elderly employee.

Mr. Jenkins grunted. "I heard you a mile away, son. No offense, but you were lumbering my way with the grace of a buffalo."

Schmidt snickered beneath his breath at the insult. He'd been called worse. He was a big man, and grace was not his middle name. "Wasn't trying to sneak up on you, sir." On the contrary, he'd made plenty of noise on purpose so as not to be mistaken for a deer or worse — a skulking trespasser. He imagined that was the real reason the older fellow was outside keeping vigil. It was a reason Schmidt happened to respect immensely.

"Figured that." The bristles of Mr. Jenkins' beard shimmered like silver in the moonlight. "You might as well drop the mister and call me Hodge. Everyone else does."

"It would be my pleasure," Schmidt agreed. "So long as you call me Schmidt."

"Don't mind if I do." The man looked pleased. "What brings you out with the wolves, son? Trouble sleeping?"

Schmidt shrugged. "More like boredom." Rolling his shoulders, he let out a sigh of contentment. Scouting around the wooded estate of the finishing school was far more to his liking than drinking tea from delicate teacups and crawling beneath fancy silk sheets afterwards. "Any sign of trouble yet?" he inquired hopefully.

Hodge shook his head. "All I've encountered so far are two deer, a fox, and one very exasperated hoot owl. He took off when he realized I was here to stay a spell." He nodded at the treetops overhead. "I reckon he didn't appreciate me tromping through his hunting grounds."

"What are you out here looking for, if you don't mind me sticking my big nose into your business?" Schmidt drew his pair of six-shooters, twirled them expertly, and took aim at a bat settling on a nearby fencepost. He made the faint popping sound of a bullet with his mouth. The startled creature gave a few clicking chirps and took wing.

"Anyone or anything that doesn't belong." The grizzled gardener's mouth settled into a flat line. "I may keep to the background most of the time, but I hear things. Enough to know that Boone and Mrs. Rachel are mighty worried right now about that pretty sister of his."

"And Lucy," Schmidt added in a harsher voice than he intended.

"And her." Hodge gave him a curious once-over. "I watch over all the girls all the time." He pursed his lips. "Can't be too careful with so many young poppets gathered in one spot like this."

Schmidt was impressed by the man's dedication to the student body as a whole. Rachel was fortunate to have both him and Boone on site to protect her growing brood of young students. "Did Boone happen to mention anything to you about the telegram Charity Powers received this morning?"

The way Hodge's back stiffened told him all he needed to know. The fellow had clearly taken it upon himself to read the message. He continued speaking as if Hodge had already owned up to his snooping. "There has to be more to the scoundrel's request than an attempt to extort a few hundred dollars. No loan shark I know of would've waited three years after a man's death to start hounding his widow. His demands would have been swift, and they would have been ruthless."

Hodge looked troubled. "You're worried about Mrs. Powers, too, aren't you?"

"I am. And Lucy as well." He couldn't put his finger on the exact reason why, only that he felt a sense of foreboding that her daughter was somehow tied up in all of this. "The demand for a couple hundred dollars feels like testing the waters, so to speak. Like someone who knows there's money to be had, but he's not yet settled on his full plan of attack." The con would be studying her behavior — how long it took her to send the first payment and how much of it she'd be able to come up with on the first pass.

Hodge shifted his hunting rifle higher on his shoulder. "And if she doesn't meet his deadline?"

"He'll tighten the screws on her." He'd issue threats. He might even go as far as to snatch her daughter and hold her for ransom. Then her mama would have no choice but to pay up, regardless of how strongly he and Boone were advising her against it. His gut told him it was only a matter of time before the ruthless Morley tried something more drastic than writing a few blustering telegrams. It was difficult to fight back when nobody knew who the despicable Morley was, what he ultimately wanted from Charity, or when he'd first show his face to her.

Hodge grimaced as he mulled over the possibilities. "What can I do to help?"

"Exactly what you're doing already," Schmidt returned brusquely. "Batten down the hatches. Shore up the locks on every door and window. Add extra ones where it makes sense. Let me pull security with you. And, by all means, report back anything suspicious you see or hear to me and Boone. We'll advise Rachel to ramp up student account-ability around the clock." No wandering off from the group to chase butterflies or pick flowers. No solo treks to attend the call of nature. No going anywhere alone for now.

The gardener gave him a mock salute. "Since these old bones aren't getting any younger, I'd prefer it if you took the first shift. I'm already an early riser, so covering the second shift will be easier for me."

Schmidt didn't care what shift he served, so long as he got to take part in the action. "As you can see, I came prepared." He twirled his pistols one more time for good measure.

Hodge chuckled. "Then I'll be heading up to the carriage house to tuck this old feller into bed for a few hours. God be with you, Mr. Bounty Hunter."

"Thank you, sir." Schmidt was touched by the man's show of fatherly concern.

Unlike Hodge, who'd appeared to be more focused on patrolling the back part of the estate, Schmidt saw more value in making rounds of the entire estate. In the event anyone unscrupulous was watching his movements, he varied his regimen each half hour. First, he patrolled the perimeter of the estate clock-wise. Then he retraced his steps and patrolled it counter clockwise. Next, he marched in a traversing motion, cutting back and forth across the front lawn, side gardens, and rear grounds in a zigzagging manner.

As he studied the ghostly outline of Rachel Cassidy's mansion and its various outbuildings, from the carriage house to the greenhouse, Schmidt was forced to admit that the finishing school had sucked him into its magical thrall. He liked it here and wasn't in nearly as big of a hurry to depart from it as he originally imagined he would be. A man could get used to sleeping on a large four-poster bed each night atop a real mattress. What a contrast his current assignment was to his many rough and tough years on the road!

Movement inside one of the second-story windows had him craning his neck for a closer look. A lone figure stepped out to the central balcony. He would have recognized her petite hourglass figure anywhere. It was the breathtaking Charity Powers. She was wearing a white, flowing gown with no coat or hat. Her breath came out in small puffs of white beneath the moonlight.

Not wishing to disturb her solitude, he stepped farther inside the shadowy tree line. A proper gentleman would have continued his patrol and moved on to give her the maximum amount of privacy, but Schmidt wasn't precisely a gentleman. He was a detective first and foremost, and sometimes snooping came with the territory.

After a few seconds, she turned off her lantern, a gesture he found odd considering how shaded the front of the house was by the towering, mature trees on the front lawn. Without a light, she was nearly as concealed by the shadows as he was. It wasn't until a few slow-moving clouds drifted past the moon that he caught a glimpse of something shiny in her hands. Something metallic. He nearly swallowed his tongue to realize she was holding a gun.

Even more concerning was the fact that she had it trained directly on the spot where he was standing. *Great jumping bullfrogs!* Sure, he was out of shooting distance, but that didn't change the fact that she'd detected his presence. What was more, he'd alarmed her enough to consider firing her weapon, an act that would unnecessarily alarm her family and all the students sleeping soundly in their dorm rooms.

"Don't shoot!" He stepped from the tree line with his arms raised. "It's only me. Schmidt."

It seemed to him that Charity took her time lowering her weapon as he moved in her direction. She waited until he was standing directly beneath the second-story balcony before lowering it to her side.

"Are you spying on me, Mr. Barnes?" She spoke in a low alto that he found entrancing. She followed the words up with a furtive glance over her shoulder, as if fearing she might wake someone despite how softly she was speaking.

"I thought you agreed to call me Schmidt," he drawled, not bothering to hide the fact that he was staring at her.

She shook her long, wavy hair back. "That's not an answer, Schmidt."

The sassy way she spoke his name tickled him to no end. She no longer sounded dazed or weepy over the discovery of who her real father was.

"I reckon I was, Charity." There was no point in denying it. She was far too smart for subterfuge. "More or less." He shot a grin in her direction that he didn't expect her to return, and she didn't. "Hodge Jenkins and I are pulling patrols of the school grounds. Correction." He held up a finger. "Hodge, you, and I are pulling patrols."

This time, he thought he saw her lips twitch, but he couldn't be sure in the darkness.

"If I bother putting on a coat and coming downstairs, will you still be there when I step out to the porch?"

His eyebrows shot upward. "I will." He wasn't due back to the carriage house for another hour. Regardless of the time, he wouldn't have told her no.

"Good. I have something I've been wanting to discuss

with you." Her voice was prim and gave no hint as to what was troubling her.

His eyebrows remained skyward for so long, it was a wonder they didn't get stuck up there. The elusive Charity Powers was actually seeking out his company? If that didn't beat all! Until this very evening, he hadn't been sure she trusted him enough to be alone with him.

She arrived too quickly for him to analyze her request to much extent. A long, dark cloak now covered her filmy white robe, though she still hadn't bothered to don a hat or gloves. "I can't think of any good reason why you and Hodge might be pulling nightly patrols," she informed tartly. "What has you so worried?"

"You," he supplied bluntly. "And Lucy."

Looking surprised, she shivered and pulled the ends of her cloak more tightly around her.

He scrubbed his gaze over her feminine outline, marveling at how tiny she was compared to him. She was so delicate that any decent gust of wind might blow her clean into the next county. Did her shivering mean she was cold or merely afraid? Should he offer to lend her his coat?

The only thing that held him back was her fiercely independent spirit. Boone had grumbled to him on a number of occasions about her refusal to accept money or gifts from her own brother.

However, Schmidt's natural supply of chivalry won the war inside his head. He couldn't bear to watch her shiver. Shrugging out of his coat, he muttered, "You're cold."

"I'm not, but thank you for your concern." She blinked up at him, giving him the pleasure of watching her long sooty eyelashes brush against her perfect, doll-like cheeks. Her coffee brown eyes were the kind that mirrored her every thought, and the number of emotions running through her right now made him downright dizzy. He detected caution, curiosity, and interest. The female kind. After her dramatic reaction the other day to discovering she was half-white, he'd been wondering if she despised all white men.

Apparently not, which was a relief.

"Are you sure? You're more than welcome to my coat." He held it out to her.

"I'm sure." Her gaze seemed to probe his very soul as he reluctantly put it back on. "You think Morley is going to show up here." It wasn't a question. Her voice was dull with acceptance, and her slender shoulders seemed to slump.

"I pray that he doesn't." Schmidt was impressed by how quickly and accurately she'd summed up the stark reality of her situation. He wished there was something he could say to reduce her fears, to offer comfort. Unfortunately, he wasn't in the business of doling out false hope.

She drew a shaky breath. "That's the real reason you're out here pulling patrols."

"Yes." It was impossible to determine if she was grateful for his assistance or just plumb scared. "I'm not the only one who's out here," he reminded in a teasing voice, striving to bolster her spirits.

She rolled her eyes. "You once called me brave, but I'm not. I only stepped outside because I cannot sleep." She bit her lower lip at the confession. "The girls were telling ghost stories earlier. Though it was only in fun, it did nothing to improve my peace of mind."

"Are you afraid of the dark?" Somehow, that didn't fit his impression of her.

She gave a short, scoffing laugh. "There are only a few things in this world I am afraid of, Mr. Barnes, but the dark isn't one of them."

The sudden snap of energy in her soft, husky voice utterly charmed him. "Schmidt," he corrected again, wondering like crazy what the few things were that scared her. If they were living, breathing creatures, he'd gladly throw a few punches at them on her behalf. "Just Schmidt." He found himself wondering a few other things about her other than her short list of fears — highly inappropriate things he was certain her brother would not approve of. Things like how well she'd fit in his arms and how her full, sassy lips would feel pressed against his.

She continued speaking as if she hadn't heard him. "Sometimes Lucy has nightmares and walks in her sleep. I was worried the ghost stories might have triggered another episode. From where I was standing on the balcony, I could see her window." Her voice was infused with motherly concern.

A mother keeping vigil was a thought that warmed his heart, even as his mind pondered the alarming possibilities of her revelation. If Lucy was prone to sleepwalking, she could end up alone and unchaperoned outside at some point. He frowned at the thought.

"Does this happen often?" He followed Charity's gaze to determine which room Lucy was sleeping in. *Argh!* He'd been so busy worrying about intruders breaching the walls of the mansion that he'd not given one thought to the possibility of a student wandering away from the safety of those walls.

"Yes and no. She might sleepwalk for three nights in a row, then go months before the next episode. Normally, she stays with me," Charity explained in a worried voice, "but she and Jessamine are staying in the Royal Room tonight. That's Pansy's niece," she explained at his puzzled look. "Rachel gave them permission, because the rest of the girls begged her to, thinking it would be a great lark. They're forever calling her The Little Princess, you see."

All Schmidt saw was that he'd made a colossal mistake in how he'd gone about his first patrol of the school grounds. He jogged to stand beneath the turret in question. "The Royal Room, you say?"

"Yes." She shot him a worried look.

"It's not like the rest of the house." His jaw clenched. "It has its own stairwell, does it not?"

She gave him a frightened nod. "I suppose it does."

"Where does it lead?" He paced back and forth in front of the turret, wishing he could see straight through the stones that formed it.

"To the library, I believe." She anxiously scanned his features. "Oh, Schmidt! Do you think—?"

"Come on!" His feet were already in motion. He reached for her hand and tugged her along as he jogged alongside the spacious home. He didn't want to picture little Lucy wandering alone in the darkened mansion, but his brain froze altogether at the thought of her unlatching a door and venturing outdoors in a semi-conscious state. If his instincts were correct, Morley might already have a henchman stationed nearby, quietly staking out the premises.

He rounded the back corner of the mansion and slowed his steps. There she was. Not wanting to alarm the small child, he paused to watch Lucy Powers move forward one tottering step at a time with her hands outstretched in front of her. Her long nightgown tangled around her legs, and she stumbled over the hem.

"My baby girl!" Charity sounded out of breath and she moved in her daughter's direction. "How can I ever thank you, Schmidt? If you hadn't thought—"

She fell abruptly silent when he caught up to her and yanked her behind him.

Something tall and dark had emerged from the woods. It loped in Lucy's direction. Schmidt withdrew his pistols and cocked them as he swiftly moved to stand between her and the approaching creature. It dawned on him that the creature was loping their way on two legs instead of four. It was a man!

"Get down!" Schmidt shouted to Charity. He shot a few rounds into the air, hoping to scare off the intruder. Instead, the man leaped on him. They crashed to the ground, grappling wildly at each other. Though Schmidt managed to get a few pistol-grip jabs in, the assailant was unaccountably stronger and faster than he'd anticipated. It took time, but he finally managed to get his hands around the scoundrel's neck while still holding on to his pistols. Before he could clamp down and squeeze, however, a gunshot went off.

It wasn't one of his own pistols. A searing pain tore through his shoulder and spread like fire down his arm. He grunted in agony and lost his grip on the thug as the man scrambled from beneath his larger frame and took off at a sprint toward the woods.

Schmidt pushed himself to his feet and staggered a few steps after him. With his one remaining good hand, he raised his pistol and fired off a few shots at the retreating figure. However, his vision was too wobbly for any real hope of accuracy.

"Schmidt!" Charity sobbed. "Oh, Schmidt!" Her soft hands fluttered over his shoulders and chest, making him wince when she grazed his injury. "You're hurt."

He was mortified to feel himself sliding to his knees.

"Where's Lucy?" He could hear a murmur of voices behind them.

"Inside. She woke up, and I shooed her back into the house. Pansy has her now." She made a sound of despair. "Boone," she called in a fearful voice. "Schmidt's hurt." She wrapped her arms around his middle while footsteps pounded down the porch stairs in their direction. However, she was unable to budge him even an inch.

A rueful chuckle escaped him. Despite his pain, she felt as good in his arms as he'd imagined she would. No, she felt better than that. She fit perfectly against him. A man could die happy in the arms of a woman like Charity Powers. She was all soft and warm, and she smelled like honey. Her scent was utterly intoxicating.

"What's so funny, you big brute?" Charity's voice grew frantic. "Don't you dare pass out on me! Don't you even think..."

Her voice faded, but the glorious way she made him feel didn't. He slumped forward in her embrace, confident she would handle matters just fine on her own if he took a little breather.

Chapter 5: Silently Falling

Rachel insisted on keeping Schmidt in the main house during his recovery to make it easier to tend his wound. She put him in the servants' quarters near the kitchen where Pansy and Mrs. Cassidy were staying. Though the accommodations were smaller and not as luxuriously outfitted as the upstairs bedchambers, Pansy had always insisted on being closest to the kitchen where her services were needed the most. Mrs. Cassidy had been equally insistent about sleeping on the main level, because her old knees didn't "enjoy the climb" as much as they used to. She still visited her daughter and granddaughter upstairs, but it wasn't an everyday occurrence.

Though it forced Charity from her own room into the busy whirl of the finishing school, she visited Schmidt every day. She felt she owed him that. He'd saved her daughter from goodness-only-knew-what at the hands of her would-be kidnapper.

The first day was a blur of doctor visits as he dug out the bullet and treated the wound against infection. Plus, the town sheriff rode by to interview the patient. Boone did most of the talking, since Schmidt was drifting in and out of consciousness. Though Charity lingered by his side afterward, he hardly seemed aware of her presence. Once, when no one else was looking, she touched the top of his hand. He turned his hand over and seemed to be trying to reach back, but it grew limp before he succeeded. His breathing evened once more into sleep.

"I'd like to have a word with you, too, Mrs. Powers, when I'm finished with Mr. Barnes." Sheriff Branch Snyder concluded his attempt at interviewing Schmidt with lots of help from Boone. He scratched a few final notes on his pad and turned his attention to her. The silver-haired lawman fixed her with an unblinking stare that was downright unnerving.

"Y-yes, sir." Apprehension flooded her chest at the prospect of being questioned by a man wearing a badge. She was a woman with a bounty on her head, and he was a man with the authority to cart her off to jail. Her anxious gaze flew to Boone's. He nodded back reassuringly.

"Perhaps you'd prefer to have this conversation in the parlor?" The sheriff swiveled on the stool where he was perched beside Schmidt's bed to direct a hopeful look at Pansy, who was keeping a watchful eye on their patient from the doorway. "There would be seats for everyone, and it would allow Mr. Barnes to get back to resting."

Though Charity gave him a mute nod, she was reluctant to leave Schmidt. He looked as big as ever, sprawled on the simple mattress and linens, but far paler than normal. It was the first time she'd seen him as vulnerable. Though his overly inquisitive nature sometimes irked her, she didn't care to see him immobilized like this. It was proof that even big, powerful men could be brought down by the shadowy creatures seeking to harm her and her daughter.

She tasted fear as she bent over Schmidt's head to speak directly in his ear — fear for him and fear for what was coming. "I'll return as soon as I can. I'm not finished with our discussion yet." She wanted to know more about his theories concerning who Morley was working for. What did the man pulling the strings ultimately want from her and her daughter? How far was he willing to go to get it?

"I'd like that." His voice was slurred with slumber, little more than a husky whisper, but it gave her comfort to hear it.

———

Pansy bustled between the kitchen and parlor, bringing tray after tray of tea, coffee, and other light refreshments. She warmed some biscuits and set out a lavish set of preserves. Today, her sugary spread included peach, blackberry, strawberry, raspberry, and blueberry preserves.

Charity watched Sheriff Snyder's gaze brighten with hungry anticipation as she artfully displayed the scrumptious snack on the coffee table in the center of their gathering.

"My Emma sent her regards when she heard I was heading out this way." He settled back in his chair with a teacup in one hand and a plate of biscuits in the other.

To Charity's dismay, he seemed in no hurry to commence her part of the interview, which meant it might be some time before she could visit Schmidt again. She swallowed an inner sigh and prayed that her daughter's valiant savior was getting some much-needed rest.

"Please send our kindest regards to her in return, sheriff." Rachel bent to murmur something in her husband's ear as she handed him a teacup. Boone, who was perched on the pianoforte bench, murmured something back and squeezed her fingers as he accepted the beverage. They exchanged a tender smile before she left the room. It was full of so much love and trust that it twisted Charity's heart-strings.

She envied what they'd found in each other, and it made her miss Jacob more than ever. *Why did you have to leave us so soon? I still need you. Lucy needs you, too.* He'd left them desperately alone in the world, vulnerable to scoundrels like Morley and whoever employed him. Sadly, Lucy wasn't even aware she lacked a father. She was an infant when the fever had taken him from this world. She had no memories of him.

Charity shifted in her seat, anxious to give her statement to the sheriff so she could return to the patient sleeping in the back room. She couldn't quite explain, even to herself, why she was so drawn to Schmidt Barnes. Maybe it was because he'd spent so many hours kicking and throwing balls with Lucy outdoors, wearing down her resistance to his rough edges. Or maybe it was because of the way he'd joined forces with Boone and Hodge to protect the lovely young students at the finishing school. Despite how much she'd balked against summoning the man into town, she felt safer with him around. Correction. She *was* safer. They all were.

As he'd demonstrated the evening before, he was the kind of man who would take bullets for those he cared about. It was no wonder Boone thought of him like a brother. Their loyalty to each other was beyond anything she'd ever witnessed among friends. She'd certainly never witnessed such devotion between men of different colors.

She was still coming to grips with the discovery about her own mix of ethnicities. However, with folks like Schmidt Barnes, Rachel Cassidy, Hodge Jenkins, Pansy, and Rachel's housekeeper, Claudette, the color of Charity's skin didn't seem to matter as much as it had in other parts of the country. What was it about this household that propelled them to demonstrate such love and acceptance toward one another? Or was it the town of Cedar Falls itself that was different from the rest of the world?

"Er, Mrs. Powers?" Sheriff Snyder cleared his throat and seemed to be waiting for her to say something.

Charity felt a rush of heat flood her cheeks at the realization that her mind had been wandering everywhere except where it needed to be. "Did you say something, sir?"

He cleared his throat again. "I was asking for your side of the story. Please describe, to the best of your abilities, what happened outside this home last night."

His piercing scrutiny was making her feel fidgety all over again, so she focused on his shiny silver star instead. "I couldn't sleep," she murmured. "I was worried about my daughter. She has nightmares, which sometimes cause her to walk in her sleep."

The sheriff looked intrigued. "About how often would you say this happens?"

"It's hard to say." She caught her lower lip between her teeth, thinking hard. "There's no real pattern, though my intuition says it's more likely to happen when she's in unfamiliar surroundings. Or when she's otherwise unsettled or even frightened. Sometimes, it happens a few days in a row. Other times, she goes months without an episode."

"Was your daughter unsettled or frightened last night, Mrs. Powers?"

"For one thing, she was sleeping in a different room

than usual." Charity's gaze skittered across the room to meet Boone's darkly concerned one. Though she had her suspicions about what had ultimately triggered her daughter's latest sleepwalking episode, she had no wish to get any of the other students into trouble by her conjectures.

Her brother nodded in encouragement, so she plowed onward. "My daughter is the youngest student here at the Cedar Falls Finishing School for Young Ladies." *Good heavens!* Where had that statement come from? She was speaking as if she and her daughter were permanent fixtures there, as if they planned to stay indefinitely.

Which we do not. The thought filled her with dread. This wasn't their home. Their home was waiting for them in Louisiana.

Boone's expression had brightened at her words, which made her heart sink all the more. Up to the point where Lucy had almost been kidnapped last night, Charity had been enjoying their visit to Texas — unexpectedly so, despite the circumstances that had forced them to extend their visit. The moment the Morley crisis was resolved, however, she would return with Lucy to their small cottage in the south and get back to earning a living as a seamstress.

She had to force those dark thoughts away in order to return her attention to Sheriff Snyder. She found him watching her with the same piercing regard he always did as he waited for her to continue.

She chose her next words carefully. "I think sometimes the older children forget that Lucy is but four-years-old. Bless her heart, she tries so hard to keep up with them. At any rate, they decided to tell ghost stories last night while she was in the room with them. She knows better than to stay and listen to nonsense like that, but I imagine she didn't wish to be regarded as a baby, so she stayed. That's what I believe sparked her nightmare last night." Charity's lower lip trembled at the horrifying memory of watching her daughter wander across the shadowy back yard in her nightgown.

"And where were you when this nightmare occurred, Mrs. Powers?"

"Outside," she admitted in a shaky voice. Guilt stabbed her at the realization that she should've never left Lucy alone with Jessamine. *What kind of mother gives a four-year-old such liberties? An irresponsible one, that's what!*

"As I said, I couldn't sleep," she continued drearily. "To be honest, I was worried about my daughter. She usually stays with me in the Parisian Room, but Rachel had given her and another student named Jessamine permission to spend the night in the Royal Room. It's something of a jest, but the other students call Lucy the Little Princess. They thought it would be a great lark for her to spend the night in a room that would make her feel like an actual princess."

Sheriff Snyder burst out laughing.

Charity gaped in surprise at him. "Did I say something funny, sir?"

It took a few tries for him to reclaim his composure. "I can't wait to tell Emma the story of the Little Princess here at the Cedar Falls Finishing School for Young Ladies. Half the town is already convinced the school is a magical place. My wife says all the girls are begging their parents to leave their regular classes, so they can start attending here." He nodded knowingly at Boone. "You and your wife might soon have a waiting list."

Boone inclined his head respectfully. "It would be our pleasure to find ourselves in such a predicament, sir. If it happens, you may rest assured we'll look into expanding our campus." He sent a curiously pleading look across the room to Charity. "Naturally, we'd have to hire more staff to make that happen."

Her hand flew to her heart. *Me? You mean me?*

"My wife is already on the hunt for a full-time music instructor. If we continue to grow the student body at the current rate, however, we'll require additional full-time instructors in French, needlepoint, and the like. You are more than welcome to help us spread the word about our hiring needs, sheriff."

Needlework! Charity couldn't think of another person more skilled with a needle and thread than herself, and she wasn't being prideful. It was her God-given gift. Though she wasn't about to accept money she hadn't earned, the possibility of coming to work for the Cedar Falls Finishing School for Young Ladies opened up a whole new world of possibilities. For one thing, Lucy would be able to continue attending the school. Then there was Mama to consider. Every instinct in her was shouting that Mama would be overjoyed at the prospect of having her small brood back together.

Branch Snyder had a twinkle in his eyes as he nodded. "All I need to do is tell my wife. It's one of the benefits of living in a small town. She'll pass the news on to her friends at the Ladies' Auxiliary. Before the end of the day, the whole town will know." He pulled out his watch fob and grimaced at it. "But I digress. Time is ticking away. I must conclude our interview so I can head to another one." He stuffed the watch fob back in his pocket. "A sheriff's work is never ended."

Charity's heartbeat sped at his announcement. His pending departure meant she would soon be able to go check on Schmidt.

"Let's see." He scowled at his notes for a moment. "Ah,

yes. Did you, by any chance, get a good look at Mr. Barnes' assailant, Mrs. Powers?"

"Not a good one, sir." She shook her head. "I'm sorry. It was dark, and I was primarily focused on getting Lucy back inside the house."

"That's understandable." The sheriff wrote something else on his notepad.

"All I can say for sure, sir, is that he was tall, broad-shouldered, and dressed in dark clothing. He might've been wearing a mask, too, because I can really only recall seeing the whites of his eyes." They'd glowed strangely and menacingly at her in the moonlight.

"Anyone big enough to put up a fight with Mr. Barnes is big indeed," the sheriff muttered. "Did you happen to note the direction he was headed when he took off?"

"South, I believe. Or southeast." She stood to face the same direction she'd been standing outside when the man had scrambled away from Schmidt and broken into a run. She pointed a finger for emphasis. "He ran that way."

Branch Snyder and Boone exchanged a troubled glance. "Towards town," they declared in unison.

Charity waited until Boone and Rachel were distracted with their goodbyes to the sheriff to slip quietly from the room. Since Lucy was still attending her art lesson, she had a few minutes to spare and knew exactly where she wanted to spend those minutes.

She stood outside the door where he was housed in the servants' quarters and raised her hand. A flood of misgivings made her hesitate before knocking.

What am I doing? I barely know the man. The best I can probably do for him is to keep walking and let him rest.

"Go on in, Mrs. Charity." Pansy's voice drifted down the dimly lit hallway.

"Oh!" Charity jolted in surprise, lowering her hand to her side. "I didn't see you." It had been so quiet in the hallway that she'd assumed she was alone.

Pansy was perched on a chair half in and half out of the kitchen, shelling peas while apparently keeping an eye on Schmidt's door. It was a rather endearing gesture on her part, one that indicated just how far Schmidt had already wormed his way into the hearts of Rachel and Boone's staff.

"Would you like some help with the peas?" It seemed like the proper thing to ask, though Charity knew it was more than that. She was stalling.

"I'm nearly finished. Go on and pay the man a visit," Pansy urged with a firm nod. "He's been asking for you."

He has? Warmth and wonder flooded Charity's insides. Without wasting any more time warring with her better judgment, she raised her hand and gave a soft knock. When their patient didn't answer, she tentatively cracked the door open and peeked inside. He appeared to be sleeping. After another moment of hesitation, she shrugged and let herself silently into the room. Maybe she would wait for a spell on the stool beside his bed. If he didn't awaken soon, she'd take her leave of him and return when he was more lucid.

"I was wondering if you'd come back." Schmidt's words wafted her way, less slurred than before.

Her heart leaped at the sound of his voice. She eagerly sought him out in the dimness and was puzzled to find his eyes were still closed. "How did you know it was me?"

"Everyone has a sound," he muttered. "Most people don't pay any attention to it, but yours is light. Graceful."

She looked suspiciously around the room but could see no reason for him to be talking out of his head in such a manner. "Did Pansy give you a nip of something to help with the pain?" She eyed the pitcher of water on the night-stand with suspicion.

He snorted. "I'm not intoxicated, if that's what you mean, darling."

Darling! She stood riveted just inside the door. For a man who claimed to be sober, he sure was spouting stuff and nonsense.

"You said you wanted to talk earlier," he pressed. "So talk."

"I, er..." She slowly glided to his bedside and took a seat on the stool, spreading her calico skirts around her. Earlier, there had been so many things she'd wanted to ask him about his investigation into her late husband's financial affairs. At the moment, however, she could only think about the oversized bounty hunter lying in bed in front of her. "How are you feeling?"

"It hurts," he growled. "Like the dickens!"

Her heart twisted in sympathy at the knowledge that he was hurting because of the risks he'd taken to save her daughter. "Thank you for what you did." She swallowed hard. "If you hadn't been there, Schmidt..." She drew a shuddery breath, unable to finish the sentence. "I-I don't know how I can ever repay you."

"With a kiss?" Though he'd yet to open his eyes, his tone had grown more hopeful.

She gasped. "What did you say?"

"You heard me," he retorted huskily.

She blushed at the teasing note in his voice, amazed that the man could jest despite the seriousness of his injury. "You're in a tremendous amount of pain, Schmidt. I'm not entirely certain you are in...full possession of your wits at the moment."

He grinned, still not opening his eyes. "Then what do you have to fear? If I'm not in full possession of my wits, who's to say I'll even remember your kiss when my wits return?"

Who, indeed? Charity gave a nervous titter. *I'll remember it, that's who.* In the absence of money, however, a kiss was the only thing she truly had to offer him. That is, unless he had trousers to be mended or a new shirt needing to be sewn.

As she parted her lips to offer such services, he reached blindly for her hand. The small, sweet gesture proved her undoing. She half rose from her stool to bend over the bed. A quick glance over her shoulder assured her that the door was still ajar, but they were alone. She blushed hotly at the realization that what she was about to do was probably the most inappropriate thing she'd ever done in her life, but she felt as drawn to him as a puppet being pulled by strings.

She leaned closer still to lightly brush her lips against his.

When she started to pull away, one large hand came off the bed to cup her head and draw her mouth back to his. This time, Schmidt did the kissing, and he did a much more thorough job of it than she had.

"Schmidt," she hissed, feeling faint. "You kept your eyes closed on purpose. You wanted me to think your condition was more delicate than it truly is."

"There is nothing delicate about me, I assure you," he scoffed. His eyes were open now, bluer than blue as he gazed deeply into her eyes.

"You're hurt," she protested in a whisper. *Because of me and my daughter.*

"I'll heal."

"I'll never forgive myself if you don't." Her voice shook as she took a seat again.

"I will." Schmidt managed to keep hold of her hand in the process. "I've never been more motivated in all my life."

She blushed as the meaning of his words sank in. "Please do, so I can scold you for taking such liberties with me," she teased, trying to lighten the tension settling between them.

"I hope you're not angling for an apology, Charity, because I'm not the least bit sorry for kissing you." His fingers tightened suggestively around hers.

She caught her breath, hardly knowing how to respond.

"If I'm being honest, I want to do it again." He raised their joined hands to his lips to kiss her fingertips with a gentleness she hadn't known he possessed before now.

She blushed harder. "While we're on the topic of honesty," she pretended to look down her nose at him, a nearly impossible task, given his size, "go on and admit you won't be forgetting our kisses anytime soon."

"Not until I cock up my toes, Charity Belle Powers."

She didn't quite know whether to be amused, flattered, or irritated over how well versed he seemed to be in every detail concerning her life. At the moment, she was experiencing a mixture of way too many emotions to name, so she gave up trying.

He lowered their joined hands to his chest. "If you prefer, I'll never speak of this again. I'll never kiss you again."

She allowed her eyelids to flutter closed at the concern in his voice and the tenderness of his touch. It had been so long since any man had made her feel so beautiful. So wanted. So cherished. The thought of living in a world that

contained no more kisses from him brought on an excruci-
ating stab of pain.

She opened her eyes and met his searching gaze while
blushing so mightily that she feared her face might explode.
"You're still in a lot of pain, Schmidt." What if it was
nothing more than the pain making him so loose-tongued at
the moment?

"I am." He brought her fingers to his mouth again,
brushing them reverently with his lips, then holding them
against his cheek. "But you made me forget it for a short
time. For that I am grateful." Despite the subterfuge he'd
employed in wrangling a few kisses from her, he wasn't
faking the pallor of his skin or the exhaustion shredding his
voice.

"Well then," she announced lightly, feeling empowered
by the sincerity of his response, "if my kisses are such strong
medicine, perhaps I should visit you again tomorrow to
administer another dose?"

He grew still for a moment, searching her face for
answers. "I'll be counting the minutes, darling."

Chapter 6: New Agency in Cedar Falls

Schmidt couldn't believe Charity Powers had actually kissed him — not only kissed him, but promised to come back and do it again! He could still feel the sweet press of her mouth against his, still detect the faint scent of honeycomb in the room. He twisted his head from side to side against the pillow, letting out a groan of frustration. If only he wasn't tied to his bed as helpless as a newborn babe! He needed his strength back so he could properly court her.

The thought dragged another groan out of him. If that didn't beat all! He'd been a rolling stone his entire life, a restless man who craved adventure. How was it possible that he was actually having thoughts of staying in one place long enough to court a woman?

But he was. There was no point in denying it. His feelings for Charity had burgeoned beyond the call of duty. The dark and lovely southern belle was, quite simply, worth taking bullets for. He'd do it again and again and again for nothing more than a kiss.

But she needed more than a human shield. She needed

more than a few stolen kisses. She needed a man who would cherish and protect her, and Lucy needed a father. Though he was more than willing to offer her his hand and his name in a marriage of convenience, he wasn't nearly as confident that she would accept his offer. Though a humble seamstress, she had more class in her little finger than many wealthier women had in their entire bodies.

She was demure and ladylike, well-mannered, and well-spoken. She was a doting mother, too, with the kind of affection for her daughter that lonely boys like him could only dream about while growing up. And she possessed a heart big enough to encompass the entire student body at the Cedar Falls Finishing School for Young Ladies. He'd discreetly watched her when she didn't think anyone else was looking.

Despite her poverty, she was always giving freely of herself and her meager possessions to others. She was constantly sewing on buttons and hemming unraveled dresses free of charge. She was constantly producing ribbons from her own sewing basket to tie back tousled hair and fasten little braids. Schmidt had even watched her stitch a small brown puppy inside the pocket of one child's pinafore to comfort her while she was away from her pet.

Charity embodied the meaning of her name, all too often waving away any assistance that came her way in return. She seemed to get more joy out of serving others than being served, even when she desperately needed help herself. Though Boone continued to grumble privately to him about her continued refusal to accept money from him, Schmidt considered it yet another reason to admire her.

It was more than admiration, though. In the short time they'd known each other, he'd come to care for her. Greatly.

Enough to want to properly court her. But would she allow him to woo her openly? And would Boone approve of it?

As if hearing his thoughts, his former business partner sauntered into the room with a cocky grin plastered across his face that practically shouted he'd been well kissed before entering.

"Well, aren't you a sorry sight?" He mockingly surveyed him with his hands propped loosely on the holsters strapped to his trousers.

Not missing a beat, Schmidt turned his face toward the wall. "If I pretend to be asleep, will you go away?" Normally, his friend's ridiculous soft spot for his wife annoyed him for the sole reason that he didn't have a woman in his own life making him feel that kind of special. But it was no longer the case, now that he had Charity and her sweet kisses making his long days of convalescing more bearable.

As anxious as he was to broach the topic of courting her, he wasn't sure now was the right time. Her brother had that glint in his eye that told Schmidt he was mulling over some theory or another concerning the case at hand.

"Probably not." Boone rested the toe of his boot on the stool beside Schmidt's bed and leaned forward to peer more closely at him. "I'll just ramble until you feel up to talking strategy again."

"I'm listening." Schmidt eagerly swiveled his head back in Boone's direction, grateful to have at least one person in his life who refused to treat him like an infernal invalid. After two full days in bed, he was well on his way to recovery.

His friend glanced out the tiny round window over the bed. It wasn't much bigger than a ship's porthole. "I might finally have a lead on that Morley scoundrel."

Schmidt's whole body went on full alert. He struggled to sit up, trying to ignore the pain shooting through his shoulder. "A little help?" What he intended as a grumble came out as more of a wheeze. It was disheartening to discover how weak his body remained.

"Patience, brother." Boone guided him to a sitting position. "Not too long ago, I had a bullet dug out of my own shoulder. It's going to take time to recover."

"We don't have time." Schmidt glared at him. "We have Charity's outlandish bounty to deal with and a would-be kidnapper on the loose with no clue whether the two events are in any way connected." He shook his head in puzzlement. Quite frankly, he was surprised an army of bounty hunters hadn't already descended en masse on Cedar Falls.

Boone sat heavily on the stool. "I think they're connected. Sheriff Snyder just paid us another visit to let us know Paisley Wilson checked in a new fellow the other night at the Cedar Falls Inn. Claims to be a southern investment banker looking to expand his property holdings out west. What's even more interesting is his size. Big and tall is how Paisley described him to the sheriff."

Schmidt had been hoping for a revelation a bit more earth-shattering. "It could be something," he mused doubtfully, "or his size could be nothing more than a coincidence."

"Paisley said she saw a face mask lying on a chair in his room. A solid black wool one."

"Half the men in town probably own one of those," Schmidt growled. Unfortunately, it didn't prove beyond a shadow of a doubt that Paisley's guest was one and the same as the mysterious Morley.

"I know what you're thinking," Boone's voice was grave, "but my gut says it's something."

Schmidt held his gaze. "Do you have eyes on him?"

"Of course. The sheriff has a deputy trailing him around town at a discreet distance."

"Any place in particular he's been visiting?"

Boone nodded. "Mostly to and from the docks and warehouses along the river."

"With or without a local tour guide?"

"He's been alone."

Schmidt grimaced. "Doesn't sound much like the actions of a highfalutin' investment banker to me."

"Nor to me," his friend agreed grimly.

"Has he met with the banker about purchasing any of these docks or warehouses?"

"According to Percy Randolf, himself? Not a single visit to the bank."

"Then we might have a lead on that Morley scoundrel, after all." Schmidt scratched his chin, knowing he was in sore need of a shave. "What I wouldn't give for five minutes alone in the room with the fellow. That would be the quickest route to getting what we need to know out of him." Albeit not the most legal means.

"I was thinking along those same lines." Boone's eyes flashed with black fire. "Once we're certain we have the correct scoundrel in our crosshairs, he's going to have a lot of answering to do for all the trouble he's put my family through. That includes you, brother."

Schmidt grinned at him. "We're not bad at this, are we?"

"This?" Boone raised a single black eyebrow as he glanced around the sparse room. "Would you care to elaborate?"

"Detective work." Schmidt gestured with both hands. "Digging for clues. Ferreting out information." It finally felt like the right time to test out the waters for building some sort of future for himself in Cedar Falls. "If I ever decide to hang up my bounty hunting hat, we could kick around the plan of opening a detective agency." He watched Boone from half-closed lids to gauge his reaction to the proposition. "Together," he added to drive the point home.

His friend gave him a sharp look. "I'm retired, remember? I'm helping my wife run a finishing school these days. And if I ever get my fill of that, the sheriff has already threatened to pin a deputy badge on me in nothing flat." Even so, his tone indicated he wasn't entirely abhorrent to the idea of detective work.

Schmidt was satisfied that he'd planted a seed in that direction. "At least admit this. You didn't think twice about calling me into town."

"You were the first man I thought of." His friend didn't hesitate. "The only man, actually."

"Because you enjoy working with me."

Boone snorted. "The word *enjoy* might be painting it a little strong. I *enjoy* spending time with my wife. You, on the other hand, are a cantankerous pain in my backside." He adopted a faraway look as he belted out a laugh. "But we always manage to get the job done despite that deplorable fact."

Schmidt snickered. "Sometimes deplorable is what it takes to get the job done. My rolled-up sleeves and your pinstriped suits aren't a bad combination. We've proven it again and again."

When he paused, Boone waved at him to continue. "I reckon this conversation has a point?"

"It does. Thought you might be interested to know I'm considering purchasing some property in Cedar Falls. That detective agency I mentioned might not be as farfetched as your eye-roll suggested it was."

Boone grew still. "Honestly? I thought you were jesting about the agency."

"And if I'm not?"

His friend let out a long, low whistle. "It would be a job that would keep us in town, eh?"

"It would." Schmidt studied him closely, wondering if he had any inkling yet about the way the wind was blowing between his best friend and his sister.

"I'd be willing to devote some prayer time toward it." Boone speared Schmidt with a warning look. "It's something I'd have to discuss with Rachel, too. Coming out of retirement isn't my decision alone. It's a decision that'll be hers and mine before it's yours and mine."

Schmidt had no objections to that. He was a patient man. However, his heart was already leaping with excitement at the possibility that he'd finally figured out a way to get his partner back. If only the good Lord would allow him to find the right parcel of property to embark upon his construction plans. "I don't suppose you have any idea where a fellow might apply for a business license around here?"

Boone's lips twitched. "The mayor's office handles those things. His name is Reggie North. Just as soon as you can hop, skip, and run again, I'll take you there myself."

"Deal." Schmidt didn't intend to wait that long, though. Just as soon as he could stagger to his feet and put one foot in front of the other, he'd be paying that visit to the mayor.

Boone made a shooting sign with his thumb and forefinger as he stood and ambled toward the door. Before turning the handle, he paused. Without looking over his shoulder, he intoned, "Are you considering putting down roots in Cedar Falls solely because of our partnership, or is there another reason?"

Schmidt decided on the spot that he wanted nothing but the truth between them. "I might have another reason. Still wrestling out the details on my knees, brother." He wasn't sure if Boone was ready to hear more on the topic yet.

"Suspected it was something like that." With that cryptic statement, Boone exited the room, leaving Schmidt to wonder if he'd already guessed the way Schmidt felt about Charity.

It was another week and a half before Schmidt felt well enough to set up an appointment to meet with Mayor North. As promised, Boone drove him there in his and Rachel's carriage.

With Schmidt's arm in a sling, it was no easy task filling out the application for his business license.

"Have you decided on a name for your new company?" Mayor Reggie North was charismatic and well spoken, a little too slicked down and spiffy for Schmidt's tastes, but an all-around likable fellow. It wasn't hard to imagine how he'd gotten elected as mayor.

"I'd like to call it the Barnes & Cassidy Detective Agency. I just need to run it past my partner first." He arched an eyebrow at Boone, hoping he wasn't jumping the gun by showing his cards like that in front of the mayor.

His friend shook his head, smirking. "Fortunately for you, I had a long talk with my wife a few nights ago about you and your latest shenanigans."

Schmidt inclined his head respectfully at the mayor.

"That would be an affirmative answer," he informed the man in a stage whisper.

"It's a mighty good thing you're still wearing a sling for sympathy," Boone growled.

"See?" Schmidt waved his good hand in the air. "A partnership made in heaven." He couldn't wait to return to the finishing school to hunt down Charity and give her the good news. She played a key role in the next phase of his plan.

As it turned out, he didn't have to hunt her down after all. She came running up to the carriage to greet him and Boone when they returned home.

"You are not going to believe this! I can hardly believe it myself!" Her words tumbled one over the other in her haste to spill them to her listeners. "Widow Wallace had me sew a dress for her last week and liked it so much, she's already told half the town. I have orders coming in right and left from ladies all over Cedar Falls. Isn't that tremendous?"

"The biggest busybody in all of Cedar Falls is serving as your trumpet?" Schmidt was overjoyed to hear it. Like him, Charity sounded as if she might no longer have plans to leave town any time soon. "Talk about bearding the dragon in her own cave!" It was a tribute to Charity's boundless empathy toward others that she'd won the support of the most difficult woman in town. His fingers itched to reach out and touch the dark, wispy curls dancing against her cheeks and temples.

Boone pretended to scowl down his nose at her. "Please assure me that all these extra side jobs will leave you with enough time to instruct our students on their needlepoint skills."

"Oh, it will, Boone! It will," she sang out. As if unable to contain her happiness any longer, she threw her arms out and twirled in a few circles. The movement made her grass green skirt fan out around her, flashing a bit of her white stockings at them. Then she set her course for the house. "I have to share my news with Rachel and Mama next. They'll want to know, too."

But you told us first.

Schmidt watched her with his heart in his eyes as she practically floated up the stairs to the front porch. She was the loveliest creature in all of Texas. In the world. In the universe. And, Lord willing, she would soon be his. He'd lost track of the number of kisses she'd given him. Every time Pansy exclaimed over how rapidly his wound was healing, he struggled not to laugh. He knew it was because of the constant sunshine and tender care Charity rained down on him when they were alone. She held his very heart in her dark, slender hands.

After leaning inside the carriage to retrieve the paperwork he'd almost left behind, he turned around to find Boone staring back and forth between Charity's retreating shoulders and him. An arrested look had crept over him.

"I love her." The words escaped Schmidt before he could think straight.

"I can see that." A furrow of concern formed in the middle of Boone's forehead. "And I'll admit, it has me worried."

Schmidt's jaw dropped. "My intentions toward her and Lucy are honorable. Surely you don't doubt that!"

"No. Nothing of the sort." His friend rubbed a hand wearily over his forehead, as if trying to manually smooth out his frown. "It's just that I never pegged you for the settling down kind of fellow."

Schmidt lounged back against the carriage, feeling rather weary himself from his premature jaunt into town. His strength was fast waning. "Well, maybe you aren't the only one who's spent the last several months changing." He gazed into the distance. "It hasn't been the same out there since you retired. I reckon I took our partnership somewhat for granted. I'd all but forgotten what it was like to be alone, and it's not the way I want to feel for the rest of my life."

Boone gave a snort that might've passed as a laugh if his expression weren't so somber. "Are you trying to say we're getting old?"

"I don't know. Older maybe?" Schmidt curled his upper lip at him. "I'm twenty-nine, Boone, and there are plenty of young bucks out there to take my place in the bounty hunting business. Like you, I've made my coin. It's time to move on to the next adventure." Money was something they rarely spoke about. They didn't have to. Both had enough to last them a lifetime. They'd made their fortunes together, and now they were about to turn over a whole new leaf together.

Boone remained silent.

"What do you say, brother?" Schmidt adopted a cajoling voice. "How about we keep the streets of Cedar Falls safe one case at a time?" He made a comical face. "Maybe two cases at a time, if the occasion calls for it."

Boone grunted. "What I say is, I can't think of too many other fellows capable of putting up with the likes of you."

Schmidt let out a hearty guffaw of triumph. "Me either."

Though Boone didn't give his brotherly permission outright, he made no move to stop Schmidt from taking his courtship attempts public that same afternoon. Despite his weakened condition, he invited Charity and Lucy to the Cedar Falls Inn for dinner, and Charity said yes. Afterward, he escorted them to the Mercantile to pick out a stick of candy for Lucy. Come Sunday morning, he especially enjoyed having Charity's hand wrapped like a warm vine around his arm when he marched her and Lucy into the church building.

He bent his head next to hers as he took his seat beside her in the pew. "Please assure me you understand that I'm trying to court you?" He kept his voice low and husky for her ears alone.

Though she continued to stare straight ahead, a smile trembled on her lips. "Believe me, Mr. Barnes. Subtlety isn't your strong suit." She folded her hands primly in her lap and added. "By now, everyone in Cedar Falls knows you're, ah..."

Lucy was wiggling and giggling softly as she and her fellow students moved into the row in front of them. A light clearing of Rachel Cassidy's throat caused the child to fall silent. She obediently took a seat and demurely smoothed her skirt over her bloomers.

Schmidt dipped his head close to Charity's once again. "Your opinion on the matter is the only one that concerns me."

Her sun-kissed cheeks took on a decidedly pink tinge. "What exactly are you asking, Mr. Barnes?" She hissed the question, still not looking at him.

"For you to court me back, I reckon." His voice dropped to an even lower note in her ear. "So I can tell you things like how beautiful you are."

She caught her breath, finally lifting her gaze shyly to meet his. "You make me feel beautiful, Schmidt." She was wearing one of her own creations, a lake blue gown with a waterfall of ruffles that had swished distractingly against the legs of his trousers on the way to their pew.

He wanted so badly to lean a few inches closer to claim her lush lips with his own. However, they were in church, and he was seated beside a woman with perfect manners. It wasn't easy, but he tamped down on his caveman instincts where she was concerned.

"So, you'll court me then?" He silently pleaded with her to give him a solid answer before the service began.

"I thought that's what we were already doing." The sparkle in her eyes told him everything else he wanted to know.

He reached for her hand, hoping she didn't mind his rugged attire too much. Nothing in the world was going to turn him into a pinstriped suit and tie wearing fellow like his business partner. In an attempt to smooth his roughest edges, however, Schmidt had gotten a haircut the day before, shaved this morning, and resisted the temptation to roll up his sleeves. He was never going to come across as refined, but he was working on his table manners, so to speak.

April

The winter winds faded into spring showers while the oddly tall guest staying at the Cedar Falls Inn continued to putter harmlessly around town. Over two months had passed since the shooting on the grounds of the finishing school. The story that made its rounds in town was that the school's nightly patrols had successfully warded off a potential burglar. Instead of damaging the school's reputation, the incident served to reinforce the fact that the safety of its students was top priority with its staff.

Though Schmidt's instincts told him that Charity and Lucy weren't out of danger yet, he began to relax in slow degrees like everyone else around them. He and Boone debated the odds that Morley was simply a demented creature. Or that he'd simply lost interest in collecting money from a woman so many hundreds of miles from home. Though Charity hadn't paid the first cent toward the money Morley claimed she owed him, no further demand notes arrived via telegram.

"I have something to show you," Schmidt announced to her after the first Sunday morning service in April. Out of the corner of his eye, he watched Boone assist his wife, mother, and niece into the waiting carriage. "It'll require walking a couple of blocks down 3rd Avenue to the livery."

Though the grass was starting to turn green from all the rain, there was still a nip in the air, a reminder that summer was in no hurry to edge spring out of the way just yet.

"If I say no," Charity taunted with a merry twinkle in her eyes, "is this one of those situations where you'll simply badger me about it until you wear me down?"

He winked at her. "You know me well, precious." So long as he lived, he was never going to get tired of her sass.

She blushed at the endearment. "Dare I ask how we'll get home if we forego our only ride?"

"I have a plan. That's all I can say right now." He gave her a tender look. "Do you trust me, dearest?"

"Mostly." She wrapped her hand around his upper arm. Tipping her face up to his, she pleaded, "Just please assure me that whatever you have planned will follow such strict lines of decorum that not even Widow Wallace will find fault with us."

He waggled his eyebrows playfully at her. "Clearly, there are some gaps in your trust, madam."

"I do trust you, Schmidt," she assured breathlessly,

"with my very life. It's my heart I'm less sure about at times."

He instantly sobered. "I would never do anything to hurt you, Charity."

"Of course you wouldn't," she cried. "That was my somewhat imperfect confession that I've never felt this way before." She gulped. "About anyone, Schmidt."

Though they'd reached the livery, he suddenly felt a little winded himself. "Are you saying...?" He shook his head. No, it wasn't possible. She'd been married before. She had a child, for pity's sake.

"I am." She paused with him outside the wide, weathered doors of the livery. "I was but seventeen when my late husband asked me to marry him. I thought I knew what love was, but we were so young at the time. We still had so much growing up to do. But now?" She gave a slight head shake, her dark eyes glistening with emotion. "Now I know what it feels like to be completely and irrevocably in love with a man who adores me in return." As she absorbed his stunned expression, a spark of mischief returned to her gaze. "You also annoy me to pieces, disturb my peace of mind, and—"

"On the bright side," he interrupted, feeling a lump form in his own throat. "We'll never be bored together, darling."

Someone threw open the livery doors behind them, and the sound of nickering horses filled the air.

She blinked at him. "Am I going to like your surprise or be annoyed to pieces all over again?"

A bark of laughter escaped him. "You're really going to make me work for your trust, eh?"

"In my defense," she sounded as breathless as he felt, "your last surprise involved a new horse who nearly toppled me over in his excitement to meet me. And before that, it was an entire litter of scrawny kittens you found on the side of the road. Although I'm not entirely certain you didn't stage that one to worm your way further into Lucy's heart. It was a completely unnecessary gesture, I assure you, since she already thinks you hung the moon and stars."

He gave one of the curls against her temple a gentle tug. "Close your eyes, darling."

"If you had any idea how fast my heart was beating right now," she warned as she squeezed her lashes against her cheeks.

"My surprise will be worth the wait. I give you my word." He guided her by her elbow farther into the livery. The surprise he had waiting for her was at the far end of the building.

"Is that so?" She gave a nervous titter. "Now I'm twice as scared."

"I'm wounded."

"Your skin is far too thick for that," she shot back.

He wished that were true, but his recent bullet wound had proved otherwise. Thankfully, the injury had healed in record time. He was no longer in a sling, and his shoulder was nearly back to full strength.

He gently maneuvered her in the direction of his surprise. "You may open your eyes now."

Her long, silky lashes fluttered upward. "Oh, Schmidt!" She pressed both hands to her cheeks at the sight of the custom-built carriage. "Is it really yours?" He'd had it painted a deep shade of green to match the cedars the town was named after. Also, because green was one of her favorite colors.

"All paid for and ready to carry you home," he assured. He was especially proud of the family crest he'd commissioned. Though she pretended otherwise, he knew how badly Charity craved respectability, not to mention how much she adored nice things. Plus, he'd been plain old hoping to impress her.

She reached out to trace the gilded gold B on a backdrop of a sword crossed with a pistol. "How did you decide on the design? The pistol I understand, Mr. Bounty Hunter, but why the sword?"

"Because the Good Book says the Word of God is sharper than any two-edged sword. I want our new detective agency to be tempered with that kind of justice and mercy."

"I love your crest, Schmidt Barnes," she declared in a tremulous voice. "I love everything it stands for, along with the man who designed it."

It was all he could do not to sweep her into his arms right then and there, but he had one more question to ask her first. "I'd like it to be your crest, too, darling." He watched her carefully for her reaction.

Her lips parted and started to tremble. "Schmidt?" There was a soft, vulnerable light in her eyes. "Are you...?"

"Yes." He took a knee on the plank floor in front of her. "I'm asking you to marry this newly retired bounty hunter. To forge a new path and make a new life with me here in Cedar Falls. You and Lucy both."

Tears spilled down her cheeks, glistening like crystals. "Oh, Schmidt!" She cupped his face in her hands, looking happier than he'd ever seen her before. "I've been praying for this moment, even when I hardly dared to hope for it."

"You had to have known we were working our way up to this, darling." He removed her hands from his cheeks and brought them to his lips. "Like you, I've never felt this way before."

"But you never said anything about marriage before today," she declared softly. "Not one word."

"Maybe I just wanted to make sure you were good and caught before I reeled you in." His voice shook with emotion, utterly eclipsing his attempt at humor.

"Well, you succeeded." The tears running down her burnished cheeks drenched his heart with more joy than he'd ever experienced.

"I'm still waiting for your answer, darling," he reminded in a rough voice.

"Yes, my dearest gunslinger. My answer is yes!" Her eyes glowed like candles as he stood and took her in his arms.

"She said yes," he shouted, lifting her feet from the ground and spinning with her. "Thank you for saying yes," he muttered against her temple as he set her feet back on the ground.

They were swarmed by townsfolk who filled the air with countless happy congratulations.

Chapter 7: Collection Time

What had started off as a few claps and hoots of encouragement from the grooms soon erupted to full-blown pandemonium.

So much for decorum! Charity found herself caught up tightly in the arms of her affianced, being twirled around and around until she was dizzy.

Happy congratulations flooded down on them like rain. She was so busy laughing, crying, and greeting their friends, that she forgave Schmidt on the spot for proposing to her in a lowly livery. It was so like him to roll up his sleeves and pour his heart out to her without any pomp and circumstance leading up to it. His devotion to her was genuine, though. His love was undeniable. And those things trumped all else.

Before she could catch her breath or her scattered emotions, he was tossing her into the driver's seat, leaping up beside her, and guiding his new carriage and team of horses from the livery. She hadn't seen the grooms hitch them up, but they must have while she'd been preoccupied with the small crowd of well-wishers.

She leaned closer to wrap her hands around Schmidt's arm, adoring the way his muscles rippled beneath her fingers as he held the reins. "Where are you taking me?"

He cast a sideways glance at her. "I'll give you one guess." He set their direction for the south part of town.

At first, she thought they were returning to the Cedar Falls Finishing School for Young Ladies, but he took them a little further west than that before bringing the team of horses to a halt. From what she could determine, they were in the middle of nowhere.

There were no buildings in sight. No pastures full of farm animals. No people. Nothing but acre after acre of raw, undeveloped countryside stretched before them. The land was thickly wooded, with only an occasional pop of clearing. A creek trickled nearby.

Charity twisted in her seat to face Schmidt. "What is this place?"

"Ours," he declared. Pride rang in his voice.

"Ours?" She gripped his arm more tightly. "Do you mean you finally bought that piece of land you've been talking about?"

"Actually, I bought two pieces of land. This one is a hundred and sixteen acres, give or take a few fence posts. I'll build you a house anywhere you want on it. The other lot is much smaller, only about half an acre. It's on Main Street, a few buildings down from the theater. That's where Boone and I will hang our shingle to the all new Barnes and Cassidy Detective Agency."

She launched herself at him, pressing happy kisses to his cheek and chin.

He pretended to cringe in mortification. "Careful, madam! Someone might see us, and finishing school instructors have a reputation to maintain. You said so yourself."

She gurgled out a laugh and gave one long blonde lock of his hair a not-so-gentle tug.

His last shred of control seemed to vanish as he hauled her into his lap.

"Schmidt!" She gave a half-hearted bleat of protest, feeling a storm of blushes creep over her face and neck.

He silenced her protest with a very tender, very thorough kiss. And then another. And then another. "I wanted to do this all morning," he confessed between kisses.

"Even while you were supposed to be listening to the pastor's sermon?" She pretended to be shocked.

"Ah, my proper little love." He kissed her again, more lingeringly than before. "You are never far from my thoughts."

At some point during their kissing, his hat had gotten knocked off. While it rested half on and half off the seat beside them, she took the opportunity to comb her fingers through his tousled hair. "I've got my work cut out with you, gunslinger." Her fingers raked through a tangle, giving it a gentle yank.

"Fair warning." He drew her closer to rest his forehead against hers. "I'm going to be a lifetime project, darling."

She loved the sound of that so much that she couldn't resist pressing another soft kiss to his lips. "I know you don't care much for suits. However, if I sew you one, will you wear it to our wedding?"

"For you? Anything." He tucked one of her curls behind her ear. "Just don't make it too pretty, alright?"

"You're going to like it. Trust me." She was already dreaming about how she would custom tailor it to his towering frame and broad shoulders. A man of his activity level would require comfort and ease of movement in anything he wore, even to their wedding.

"I do trust you." His voice grew thick. "With my wardrobe, my heart, and my life."

It was humbling to hear a man of his strength and means make such a declaration. Would he trust her with the truth on another matter, though? She fell silent as she mulled over the question she'd been pining to ask him for weeks.

"Do you mind if I ask you something difficult, Schmidt?"

He nipped a kiss at the side of her mouth. "I have nothing to hide from you, sweetheart."

"Do you think I'm pretty?" She held her breath as she waited for his response.

"What?" He drew away in surprise to get a better look at her. His thick eyebrows were arched with incredulity. He looked like he was trying to decide whether to laugh or scowl. "Are you being serious?"

"Of course I'm being serious!" She wrinkled her nose at him. "I'm a woman, Schmidt!"

"And I am mighty, mighty, mighty glad that you are." He punctuated each mighty with a gentle kiss — one on her nose, one on her cheek, and one on her lips.

"I'm a different color than you," she pressed. "A very different color." So was Lucy. He was never going to look like her daughter's blood relative. All their lives together, they'd be peppered with curious stares and questions. She needed to know that he'd considered such things carefully before becoming her husband.

He drew one long finger down her cheek before answering. "So is my brother, Boone, and my other mother. Ask them how much of a problem it's been for us." His gaze softened as he leaned in to nuzzle her ear. "I don't know what answer you're looking for, but I don't particularly care what color you are. I'm in love with you, sweetheart. The woman who just agreed to put up with me and my rough edges for the rest of my days. The fact that you happen to look like a goddess is my everlasting good fortune."

A goddess? She caught her breath. "So you *do* think I'm pretty!"

"I think you're perfect." He gave her an incredulous look. "Now can we please get back to kissing?"

She chuckled happily as one of her biggest and last fears slipped away. *Oh, Mama! I might just have to forgive you for marrying a white man after all.* She wrapped her arms around her favorite gunslinger's neck. "I love you so much, Schmidt." The way she felt about him was so dizzying and overwhelming that she might never fully get used to it.

"Now that." He cupped her face between his large hands, looking genuinely puzzled as he searched her features. "That's the part I'm still trying to understand." His blue gaze burned into hers. "What did I ever do to deserve you, Charity?" He swallowed hard. "You don't have to answer that if you don't want to. I already know I don't deserve you, but I promise to spend the rest of my life trying to become a man who does. With the Lord's help, of course."

Before she could formulate an answer worthy of such a heartfelt confession, one of his horses whinnied loudly. The mare tossed her head in alarm, grazing the neck of the reddish-brown gelding hitched beside her.

"What in the world?" Schmidt leaned away from Charity, trying to determine what was agitating the creature.

Something was wrong. Charity could feel it. A cold sensation formed in the pit of her belly and grew. Seconds later, the seat vibrated beneath them. She twisted her head around the side of the carriage to peer behind them. What she saw made her heart skip a few beats.

"There are men coming our way!" They were dressed in solid black, just like the man who'd tried to kidnap Lucy. Even though it was springtime, they were wearing the same terrifying masks, right down to the eye holes. "Three of them. No. Four." Her breath grew ragged at the realization that she and Schmidt were sorely outnumbered. "What do you think they want this time?"

"Doesn't matter," he snarled. "Whatever it is, they can't have it. I won't let them." He angled his head urgently at the carriage. "I need you to hop down and climb inside the carriage, darling. It'll be safer for you that way."

"No!" She couldn't bear the thought of leaving him even more outnumbered. "I can shoot. You know I can. Give me one of your pistols." She mentally berated herself for removing her own small pistol from her reticule, having always considered it sacrilegious to carry a weapon to church. It was a mistake she would never make again.

Schmidt's mouth twisted in frustration as he removed a small pistol from his boot, a third one she hadn't even known he was carrying. "May the good Lord forgive me for not keeping you safer. My gut told me the danger wasn't over. I should've listened to it."

As he pressed the pistol into her hands, something inside her snapped. In that moment, she realized the regret in his voice bothered her more than the four men barreling on horseback in their direction.

As he lifted the reins and urged his team of horses forward, anger filled her mouth and trickled down her throat, fingering its way to her belly. She still had no idea who their nameless, faceless pursuers were. However, if they wanted a fight, she planned to help Schmidt deliver one those cowards wouldn't soon forget.

She inquired between gritted teeth. "Do you have extra bullets?"

"In the metal box under the seat." He didn't glance her way again, trusting her to locate them on her own as he urged the horses to go faster. The men on horseback thundered ever closer.

Charity risked another peek at them. The horses they rode were kicking up a cloud of dust with their hooves. She was not surprised to see how quickly they were gaining on the carriage.

"What's our plan, gunslinger?" A strange sense of peace settled over her. It was odd, considering how badly the odds were stacked against them. However, she'd never before wanted so badly to fight back, maybe because she'd never before had so much worth fighting for.

"I need you to take over the reins. Can you do that, darling?"

"I can," she assured fiercely. "Like Lucy, I'm small but mighty."

"Yes, you are." He transferred the reins to her and retrieved the pistol he'd given her. "Hold the horses steady. I'm going to use the carriage as a shield and try to pick them off before they reach us. It's our best chance."

You mean our only chance. Her fevered brain filled in the words he'd left unsaid. She gripped the reins tighter. "I'm ready, Schmidt."

He nodded and crouched in the seat beside her to peer over the top of the carriage. "I love you, Charity. Until my last breath and beyond, darling."

"You'd better, since we're about to be wed." She gasped

out the words before falling silent. It took nearly every ounce of her energy to hold all four galloping horses steady.

With a chuckle, Schmidt raised his pistols. She heard the double crack of gunfire as he aimed and fired both of them at the same time. The sound made the horses scream in terror and dig in their hooves all the harder into the hard-packed road.

Charity's vision clouded, and the strain on her forearms reached screaming levels. *Just a little longer.* She chanted the words over and over in her mind. *Just a little longer. I can do it. I must. Help us, Lord!*

When she was no longer certain her energy would last a minute longer, Boone's voice bellowed over the terrified screams of their horses, filling her ears. "Whoa! Whoa there! Who-o-o-o-o-a!"

She wondered if she was dreaming, she'd passed out, or worse — if she'd been shot and was already dead.

"Boone?" Hot tears streaked her cheeks. "I can't hold on much longer," she wept.

"I'm here," he assured in a disembodied voice.

Moments later, he drew abreast of their speeding carriage. He was riding a dark horse. "Whoa there! Who-o-o-o-o-a!" From the corner of her eye, she watched him slide his boots from his stirrups and rise to crouch on the saddle. Then he leaped in her direction.

As the reins slid from her numb fingers, he was there to snatch them up. "Whoa, there! Who-o-o-o-o-a!" His sleeves were rolled up, and his dark arms bulged from the effort of tugging Schmidt's team of horses back into submission.

Charity's hands could no longer grip anything, so she leaned against his strong shoulder and braced her feet against the floor for leverage.

The road ahead was coming to a dead end, and a line of

cedar trees loomed ominously beyond it. If Boone couldn't halt the carriage in time, they would crash into the ungiving wall of tree trunks.

"Please, God," Charity whispered one last time.

The horses abruptly slowed to a canter and then to a walk.

"Good job," Boone called to the creatures, this time in a much gentler voice as he started to turn them. They made a half circle and shuddered to a halt at long last.

All four horses were slick with sweat and trembling with fear and exertion. Boone continued to speak quietly to calm them.

Schmidt lowered himself heavily to the seat beside Charity. He shoved his pistols back in their holsters. "Are you alright, darling?" His hands urgently moved across her shoulders and down her arms. "Say something. I beg you." His voice cracked.

"I cannot feel my arms." Her voice was shaking so badly she could barely form the words.

"Were you shot?" His examination of her limbs grew more frantic.

"N-no." She had no idea why her teeth were chattering. "And y-you?"

"I'm fine." He continued to probe her wrists and hands for broken bones. "So help me, if you're injured in any way..."

"The feeling seems to b-be coming b-back." She finally managed to wiggle a few fingers.

"She's in shock." Boone shrugged out of his vest and draped it around her shoulders.

Since Schmidt wasn't wearing either a vest or a jacket, he wrapped his arms around her and drew her against his chest.

She burrowed closer, shivering. Together, they watched a new swarm of riders crest the short knoll behind them and fan out like ants. This group was wearing deputy badges. They converged on the men in black, quickly surrounding them, but not before Charity noted that all four of them were writhing on the ground.

"They're n-not dead," she noted in a weak voice.

"Naw, I only winged them." Schmidt pressed his cheek to hers. "Didn't want to risk being hauled away in cuffs right before our wedding."

"You are something else, gunslinger." She reached up to tangle her fingers in his hair. His Stetson was long gone.

"I'm all yours. That's what I am, darling." His arms tightened around her.

Boone cleared his throat suggestively. "I'm still here, you two lovebirds."

Schmidt made a scoffing sound. "For months, I've had to stomach your endless billing and cooing with your bride. It's your turn to suffer."

Chuckling, Charity peeked over at her brother. "Thank you for coming. I don't know how you knew we needed you or where to find us, for that matter, but I will be forever grateful."

"I'd rather you give God the glory for that." He let out a heavy breath. "Schmidt told me about the carriage he'd purchased for you and how he planned to bring you by his property. That's how I knew where to find you." His voice turned dry. "I'm guessing you gave him the answer he was hoping for to the question he asked you first?"

"Did I?" she teased softly for Schmidt's benefit.

"The perfect answer," he assured huskily, "followed by the perfect kisses."

"Still here," Boone groaned as Schmidt kissed a noisy trail down her cheek.

Charity shivered again, this time from the delicious warmth spreading through her. "You still didn't tell us how you knew we needed you *now*."

"That was a little trickier." Boone's voice grew grim again. "Suffice to say we had a breakthrough in the case. A big enough breakthrough that the sheriff deemed it worthy of sending a precautionary posse of lawmen to escort the two of you back to town."

"What sort of breakthrough?" Schmidt's voice was muffled against her hair.

"For one thing, we finally figured out who Morley is."

Charity grew still in Schmidt's embrace, sensing she wasn't going to like what her brother said next. "Who?"

"One of Mayor Dunaway's hired hands. So were the three other thugs he sent as reinforcements from Lafayette to speed Morley's mission along."

She frowned in confusion. "What could my half-brother possibly have against Lucy and me? We don't even know the man!" They'd not once met in person, and she'd only recently learned they were related.

"It's a good thing you're already sitting down," Boone's voice grew even chillier. "Seems as if he built a new home for his wife and sold the old one a few months ago. Unfortunately for him, your late father must have penned a new will right before he passed away and hid it in the house. It was discovered by the new owners and made public."

"He was my father, too," she mused quietly. After falling in love with Schmidt, it had become easier to accept that part of her past.

"A man who loved you enough to mention you in his last will and testament."

"Me?" This was news to Charity.

"Yes. He split his wealth evenly between you and your half brother. Your portion was to be awarded to you at the time you were wed."

"Why wasn't it?" Her eyes widened at the realization that five years had passed since she'd first pledged herself to Jacob Powers.

"Because your half-brother had been spending money so lavishly that handing over your half would have left him bankrupt. So he concocted the story that Jacob owed him money and tasked Morley with hounding you for it. He hoped to frighten you away from Louisiana for good."

"Well, it worked," she gasped. "Why couldn't he leave it at that?"

"Apparently, he suffers from paranoia. Ultimately, he decided that you and Lucy would remain a threat to his fortune as long as you remained alive."

Charity's insides turned icy. "He wasn't simply trying to scare us. He intended to eliminate us!"

"I'm afraid so."

Her face flamed with fury. "It's a good thing he won't require any cash where he's going, because I'm going to be tempted to pick his bones clean in court for what he put us through!"

Schmidt kissed her earlobe. "Will you listen to her, Boone? Already sounding like the proper wife of a bounty hunter."

Boone made a scoffing sound. "If you meant to say a bounty hunter's sister, then I agree."

"Naw, I'm pretty sure I meant to say wife." Schmidt's wink behind Boone's back told her that he was enjoying needling her brother.

Chapter 8: More than Meets the Eye

Boone, Schmidt, and Charity returned to the Cedar Falls Finishing School for Young Ladies all dusty and sweaty but exultant.

Rachel flung open the front door of the mansion and ran down the stairs to throw herself in her husband's arms. "You made it back," she breathed in a voice infused with emotion.

"I'll always come back to you, dearest." He pressed her cheek to his shoulder and smoothed a hand over her glorious auburn tresses. "I'm sorry to have worried you, but I had to ensure these two lovebirds made it back in one piece for their wedding."

"Did you say wedding?" Rachel disengaged herself from Boone's embrace to hold both hands out to Charity. "I am so happy for you."

Charity smiled from the haven of Schmidt's embrace. "I'm having trouble lifting my arms at the moment, but I promise to deliver you a hug as soon as I am able."

"What happened?" Rachel smoothed her hands in agitation down her silk skirt. "On second thought, how about you come inside for some refreshments while you tell your story?"

She gasped her way through their outrageous tale of danger and intrigue. "The bounty hunter's sister," she repeated in awe, looking at Charity with new eyes. "I knew you could sew like a magician, but I had no idea you were capable of such legendary exploits. Just wait until our students hear of this. They'll never stop singing your praises."

"Pshaw!" Charity bashfully lowered her gaze. "I did nothing more than you would've done in my shoes. You love Boone the way I love Schmidt."

"That I do, sister dearest." Rachel rang for a fresh pot of tea.

Charity raised her damp gaze to the lovely head-mistress. "You called me sister," she said dreamily. It was the first time she could recall Rachel doing so.

"That I did." The glow in the elegant young woman's eyes warmed Charity all the way to her toes. "The sister of my bounty hunter is my sister as well."

The following week was so busy that Charity and Schmidt were unable to visit his land again until after the Sunday morning service.

Schmidt kept Lucy's hand tightly clasped in his as she pranced out the front door between him and Charity. The child was a bundle of energy. She rarely walked anywhere. She skipped, hopped or danced her way through life. Even her long banana curls never stopped moving. They bounced with every step she took.

He caught Charity's eye. "It's like trying to hold on to a frisky tiger. Has she always been like this?"

"Always," his affianced sighed, looking like she was struggling to hold in a chuckle. "Enrolling her at the finishing school has given me a much-needed break. It was much harder keeping up with my sewing commitments before that." She had on her ruffled blue gown that always made him think of waterfalls. No less than three church ladies had stopped her this morning to see if she'd make them one in a different color.

"I have an idea how we might burn off a little more of her energy." He watched in bemusement as the lips of the dark little princess between them silently moved to keep count of her steps. Unless he was mistaken, the minx was waltzing her way to the carriage. Her pale pink bloomers peeked out from beneath her lacy pink dress with each sashaying step.

Charity's eyes sparkled into his. "You do realize she's wearing her second best dress?"

He waggled his eyebrows back at her. "I happen to know a really great seamstress." It almost felt wrong to call her that. She was so much more than a seamstress. She had a real gift for turning fabric and thread into museum-worthy displays. He couldn't have been more admiring of her talent.

Charity bit her lower lip. "Very well. Where do you suggest we let the tiger run next?"

Lucy must have overheard the comment, because she emitted a low growling sound. "I'm a tiger! Grrr!" Her dancing halted, and she lowered her head closer to the ground, giving the nearest family her best menacing glower.

Charity gave her daughter's hand a firm squeeze. "Manners, Lucy!"

Lucy straightened. "But I'm a nice tiger, Mama! I wasn't growling too loudly, was I?"

Charity shot a pleading look at Schmidt. "I'm open to any reasonable suggestions that won't require a complete replacement of her outfit."

He angled his head toward the road leading away from town. "How about we take another look at our land?"

"Our land." Her expression softened as she repeated his words. "I really love how that rolls off my tongue."

He held her gaze, cocking his head at her. "You sure you don't mind driving out there so soon after...?" Not wanting to alarm Lucy, he didn't finish the question.

She helped him lift Lucy onto the driver's seat so they could keep her between them. Though she kept her voice low, her expression grew fierce as she declared, "I'm not going to let some two-bit thugs frighten us away from our very own slice of heaven."

"That's my girl." He kissed her with his eyes as he handed her up after Lucy.

"All yours," she assured in a breathy voice as she settled her skirt around her ankles. "Besides, I can't wait to see where you're going to build our home."

As he climbed in to take hold of the reins, he gazed fondly at the two beautiful ladies he was about to drive through town. "I told you the exact spot was yours to decide, darling."

Charity reached around her daughter to rest a hand on his upper arm as they rolled from the parking lot. "My first tour of it was a little too eventful for decisions like that. Maybe we can pinpoint the perfect spot today." She smiled down at Lucy. "Who knows? Maybe a certain little tiger will help us narrow down the best areas to run and play."

He cast a curious sideways look at her. "Hopefully a

place suitable for more than one tiger to play." They hadn't yet spoken about starting a family together, but he'd been hoping in that direction.

Her dark lashes fluttered against her cheeks. "Do you want children, Schmidt?"

"Clearly." He couldn't believe she felt the need to ask. "I'm marrying a woman with a child, aren't I?"

"I was referring to more." Her breathing grew shallow. "You once told me you were a restless man, and children are a tremendous responsibility. Are you sure you're ready for—"

"Yes, I want more," he interrupted evenly. *With you, darling.* He added the rest in his head.

Whatever she read in his expression made her glance away. "It won't be easy wrestling more than one tiger at a time."

He snorted. "Nothing about my life has been easy, darling. I'm not looking for easy." If life had taught him anything at all, it was that everything worth having required a little work. Sometimes a lot of work. And starting a family with Charity was most definitely something worth having.

They reached the turn off to the property he'd purchased. Instead of rolling past it like he had the last time, he gingerly drove the carriage into a grassy clearing before halting the horses.

He leaped down and reached for Lucy. She was so busy gaping at their surroundings that she practically fell into his arms. Her mouth rounded in a silent O of wonder.

All Schmidt had to do was plop her on her feet. Her tiny boots immediately started to move as she raced off to explore the nearest patch of wildflowers.

"Stay where I can see you, sweetheart," her mother

called after her as she allowed Schmidt to lift her down next.

His heart swelled with pride as he swung her in a slow circle. Even after he set her back on her feet, he was in no hurry to let her go. Instead of following after Lucy, he cuddled Charity closer. After being alone for so long, he felt like the most blessed man in Texas to finally have a family to call his own.

"What are you thinking?" She tipped her face up to his.

"That I have everything I've ever wanted." He reached up to trace her lower lip with his thumb.

"Everything?" Her voice was teasing. "Didn't you just finish telling me you wanted more?"

He swooped in for a kiss, longing to get another sample of the sass on her lips. "Despite all your manners, you're as much of a minx as Lucy."

She kissed him back. "Something tells me you were no angel as a child, either."

He snickered instead of defending himself. "So what you're saying is, starting a family with you is going to be nothing but trouble?" He nuzzled the corner of her mouth, adoring the soft sigh it drew from her.

"It won't be *all* trouble," she assured in a laughing voice. "But, yes. Some."

"Well, you picked the right fellow to start a family with." He gazed adoringly down at her. "Bounty hunters have a tendency to run toward trouble, darling. Not away from it."

She drenched him with a happy smile. "So long as you understand what you're getting into."

"I do. I want it all. I want to marry you, start a family together, and this." He dove in for another kiss to drive his point home.

Thank you for reading
The Bounty Hunter's Sister.

A tall, broad-shouldered, and deliciously unwed blacksmith moves to Cedar Falls to the joy of all the marriage-minded ladies. However, the only woman he can't stop thinking about has made it clear she's not in the market for a husband in
Rescuing the Blacksmith.

Sneak Preview: Rescuing the Blacksmith

November, 1867

*O**nly six more weeks until Christmas.*

It was Laura Bennett's least favorite time of the year. December was full of too many bittersweet memories about her life before the war— before losing her fiancé during a battle in Charleston and before losing her father during a subsequent battle in Atlanta. Her mother had succumbed to a fever shortly afterward. Or a broken heart, depending on who was telling the tale.

Laura was certain the only reason she'd survived the triple tragedy was because of her grandparents' swift intervention. Four years ago today, they'd whisked her by train to their cozy hometown of Cedar Falls, Texas.

And the rest was...well, she was still figuring out the rest. One day at a time.

She rubbed her hands up and down her arms as she took a quick survey of her non-black gowns. As it turned out, there were only two of them — the green velvet one and a cheerful cotton floral one. It was the last gown her dearly departed Peter had seen her in before marching off to that fateful battle in Charleston. Though she never planned to wear the gown again, she'd not been able to bring herself to part with it. The lovely pale pink garment held too many bittersweet memories. Like a flower that had long since dried between the pages of a book, she kept it folded deep within her gown collection.

With a sigh, she reached for the velvet gown instead. It felt like a compromise of sorts. The fabric was dark enough for mourning but as green as a Christmas garland. Plus, it was a gift from two people she loved.

There was no guarantee that it would put her in a festive mood, but she went through the motions of changing into the lovely gown, anyway. Standing in front of the dressing mirror, she felt a whole new kind of apology spring to her lips.

I'm so, so, so sorry, Peter. It felt wrong — wronger than wrong — to be dressing for a town-wide celebration while his body lay cold in the ground of a southern cemetery. *This is simply to make my grandmother happy. I won't forget your sacrifice. Not for one second this evening.*

She pulled the pins from her updo, brushed out her long brunette hair, and tucked it into a fresh twist against the back of her neck. There was no time to crimp the stray wisps of hair at her temples into curls. She settled for dampening them in the wash basin and winding them around her finger. They would dry in gentle waves around her face. It was the best she could do on such short notice. There was nothing she could do about how pale her cheeks were or how loose the gown hung on her too-thin frame.

Thankfully, her winter cloak helped hide the looseness. She set a felt hat at a jaunty angle over her hair and pulled on her gloves.

On her walk down the hallway toward the stairs, she heard a scraping sound outside the balcony doors.

"Oh, dear! I forgot all about you." Feeling guilty about spending the last half hour so immersed in melancholy, Laura hurried to open the door on the right and let Button back inside. "There you are, my fierce warrior cat."

She wrinkled her nose at the bony remains he'd deposited on the doorstep. He'd picked the little carcass clean. She shivered and made a mental note to clean up the mess in the morning.

Button pranced like a little prince down the hallway in front of her with his tail held high. They reached the stairs, and she paused at the landing. Button paused beside her, looking up at her expectantly.

She pressed a finger to her lips, hoping he understood the universal sign to hush. Her grandparents were in the foyer below, helping each other layer up to brave the outdoor temperatures. Neither of them had yet noticed her presence.

She and Button made their way down the long stairwell together. To his credit, the cat kept silent as she'd requested. The only sound was the soft rustle of Laura's velvet skirt against the wooden steps behind her.

Her grandmother suddenly grew still. Though her back was to Laura, she turned her head sideways, listening. Digging her cane into the large Persian rug at her feet, she pivoted around. A black fur cloak was now covering the top half of her burgundy gown.

"My dearest Laura!" Her tea root-colored eyes glinted with unshed tears. "I couldn't be happier that you've decided to attend the tree lighting with us."

Evan Bennett made a limping pivot to stand shoulder-to-shoulder with his wife. He reached up to tip his

Stetson gallantly toward Laura as she finished descending the stairs. His silvery hair waved out from beneath the brim in the back, brushing the black wool collar of his overcoat.

"I'm a lucky fellow indeed to be driving the two loveliest ladies in Cedar Falls around this evening." He couldn't have looked or sounded prouder. Despite the gout that caused endless amounts of pain in his left foot, he straightened to his full, towering height. Back in his prime, he'd stood six feet three inches. Age and gravity had taken their toll on his handsome frame. However, he was still a good six feet tall.

Fighting tears, Laura reached for the arm he was crooking at her and curled her hand around it. "Coming with you this evening is the least I can do to show my gratitude for your hospitality these past four years."

"Pshaw! Our home will forever be open to you, dearest," her grandmother assured with a tremulous smile. "But that's not why I invited you. Simply put, no Christmas tree lighting ceremony would feel complete without our entire family present." She fluttered a hand at the two of them. "Our number may be small, but I couldn't be more thankful for both of you."

Before she started weeping, Laura strove to inject a lighter note into the conversation. "Technically, we're up to four." Her voice shook a little from her effort to control her emotions. "Not only did Button protect me from a horrid mouse on the second floor, like a perfect gentleman, he escorted me down the stairs."

The three of them shared a chuckle on their way out the front door. Her grandfather already had a regal team of reddish-brown quarter horses hitched to his elegant black carriage. After helping her and her grandmother inside the carriage, he shut the door behind them and climbed into the driver's seat.

Since they lived so close to town, their drive to the downtown area of Cedar Falls didn't take long. Evan Bennett slowed the horses to a walk as he drove them down Main Street toward Town Square.

Both sides of the street were packed with pedestrians. Families with children walked hand-in-hand — five and six people deep in some cases. Mothers held babies. Courting couples and newlyweds had their arms locked.

A stringed quartet played holiday carols from the gazebo in the square. An enormous Christmas tree stood beside it, decked out with ribbons and ornaments. Though the ceremony the town had planned wouldn't have worked on a windy evening, the air had grown still enough to coop-erate — just like Grandmother had predicted. An enormous star made of unlit candles had been mounted to the top of the tree. Six more round tiers of unlit candles encircled the branches.

Clara Bennett peered out the window of the carriage in excitement. "It's so festive. They really outdid themselves this time," she sighed, twisting to catch Laura's gaze. "Nothing is more lovely than the sight of you in your velvet dress, though. Absolutely nothing!"

Laura smoothed her gloved hands over the full skirt. "Thank you, ma'am." The velvet fabric was not simply beautiful. It was doing a wonderful job of keeping her legs warm.

Their carriage halted in a long line of vehicles waiting to reach Town Square.

Moments later, her grandfather opened the carriage door. "This is as close as we're going to get, I'm afraid. If you don't mind walking the rest of the way, I'll go park the carriage at the livery a few doors down."

"We don't mind one bit." Her grandmother rose and leaned into his embrace, chuckling girlishly as he swung her down like she weighed next to nothing. "Thank you, Evan." She patted his shoulder affectionately.

For an answer, he gave her a peck on the cheek.

Her grandmother shivered. "That may very well be the coldest kiss you've ever given me, dearest." She added in a softer voice, "But it's from the warmest heart in Texas."

Their sweet banter sent a pang of envy through Laura, catching her off guard. She gazed around the busy street as her grandfather assisted her to the ground, trying not to think about how much their conversation made her miss Peter.

Her favorite broad-shouldered train conductor had enjoyed mixing his displays of affection with humor. Teasing her had been one of his biggest joys. When he'd fallen in battle, however, her laughter seemed to have died with him.

Her gaze flitted from face to face in the crowd, desperately seeking something. She didn't know what it was until she found it.

Until she found *him*, to be more precise — Wyatt James, the new blacksmith in town whom she'd met for the first time only hours earlier.

He was standing alone by one of the light posts on the side of the road. He was a big man, bigger than her fiancé had been — a good two or three inches taller, for sure, with a broader chest and shoulders. His size was probably the only reason she'd picked him out of the noisy, writhing crowd.

The look in his eyes, however, was what made her gaze linger on him. She would recognize that hooded look of torment anywhere. The poor man looked as sad and as miserable as she felt. She could sense it from the twenty yards or so that separated them.

Like her, he must have lost someone. Someone important to him. Someone whose absence made the holidays just shy of unbearable. He wasn't enjoying the festive sights and sounds around them any more than she was.

His chest rose and fell as he shifted from one boot to the next. His stance indicated that he was ready to bolt. He half turned toward the street, preparing to make his getaway.

A dignified man in a suit and black top hat approached him, stopping between him and the street, effectively cutting off his escape route.

Laura's eyes widened as she recognized Mayor Reggie North. He shook hands with the blacksmith, saying something jovial while miming the swing of a large hammer through the air, clearly discussing something related to Mr. James' job.

Though she knew she was staring, she had a difficult time tearing her gaze away from the two men. According to her grandmother, all the unmarried ladies in town were in a tizzy over the blacksmith. And no wonder. Like many towns across America, Cedar Falls had suffered the loss of countless young men during the war, rendering them desperately short of unattached bachelors.

Wyatt James fell solidly into that hallowed category with his undeniable singleness. And impressive size. And the fact that he owned his own business. Interestingly enough, he appeared in no hurry to change his bachelor status. If her grandmother's sources were correct, he'd turned down nearly every invitation he'd received to various social gatherings this holiday season, to the dismay of all the hopeful young ladies.

And now I know why.

Not that it was any of Laura's business, but the new blacksmith of Cedar Falls was grieving. She was sure of it.

Her grandmother clutched her arm as her grandfather drove their carriage toward the livery. "I told Evan we'd carve out a spot for us by the tree." She towed Laura through the thick tide of humanity covering the sidewalk, bringing them closer to the mayor and blacksmith.

"Oh, there's Mayor North," her grandmother exclaimed. "We should stop and say hello. I've been meaning to ask him..."

The rest of what she said was lost on Laura as Wyatt James turned his head in their direction. His rugged features were chapped red, and the auburn hair poking from beneath his Stetson was tousled by the wind. His deep blue-green gaze latched onto hers and held for a breathless moment.

It was like one lost soul finding another lost soul and clinging to them for dear life. Awareness slammed into Laura — so powerfully that it was suddenly harder to breathe. She could taste it and feel it. For a second or two, she almost felt like she was drowning. Then it was over.

Though Mr. James continued to watch her approach, his expression grew hooded. The sense of one soul reaching out to another faded. It was as if he'd deliberately withdrawn from her.

Her grandmother greeted the mayor merrily and jumped right into the introductions. "Mr. Mayor, you've already met my granddaughter. Mr. James, you have not."

Laura didn't bother setting her straight. She knew better than to interrupt her grandmother when she had her teeth sunk into a conversation like a hungry fox with a juicy bone. "It's my greatest pleasure to introduce my darling granddaughter to you, Laura Bennett. Laura dearest, this is Wyatt James, the most skilled blacksmith who's ever graced the streets of Cedar Falls. We are most fortunate to have a man of his skills in town."

Laura watched Mr. James withdraw even more inside himself. He spoke polite words and held her hand for as short a time as possible without appearing rude. No doubt he assumed that her grandmother was purposely dangling yet another eligible young woman beneath his nose, hoping she'd capture his bachelor interest.

As her grandmother babbled out an explanation of her granddaughter's many charitable endeavors across town, Laura rolled her eyes at the blacksmith without thinking.

His gaze lost some of its melancholy, momentarily sharpening with interest on her. An acute sense of aware-ness zinged between them again.

She glanced away in confusion, not having intended to do anything worthy of his notice. As soon as her grand-mother paused to take a breath, she tugged on her arm. "It was nice to meet you, Mr. James, and wonderful as always to see you again, Mr. Mayor. We'd best be on our way before Grandfather thinks we lost our way to the tree light-ing." She nodded at the two men and all but dragged her grandmother past them.

Maybe it was her imagination, but she could practically feel Wyatt James' gaze scorching her shoulder blades as she hastened to put distance between them, something that was neither a quick nor an easy task on the crowded sidewalk.

"Good gracious, child!" Clara Bennett gave her a scan-dalized look once they were out of earshot. "Your behavior with the mayor and blacksmith bordered on rudeness."

Laura snorted. "If you were hoping I'd catch Mr. James'

attention, lingering for endless small talk would've been unwise. I imagine he's accustomed to being fawned over."

"How right you are!" Her grandmother's smile returned in full force. "On second thought, you played your hand quite nicely back there, my dear."

Laura didn't bother telling her she hadn't been playing at all. She was no more interested in capturing the blacksmith's attention than he was in having it captured.

Like her, he was in mourning. She'd done them both a favor by ending their encounter early.

Her grandfather joined them when they reached the Christmas tree. "There you are!" He shimmied his way between them, proudly taking their arms.

Only a handful of minutes later, the mayor made his way to the grandstand. "Good evening, folks! On behalf of the Cedar Falls council, it is my greatest honor and pleasure to welcome you to this evening's tree lighting ceremony. I hope you will linger for a few minutes afterward for a very important, very exciting announcement. And now, without any further ado..." He motioned for the stringed quartet to start playing again.

The musicians led the crowd in a few rousing Christmas carols that had hands clapping and feet stomping. Then the music slowed and grew softer as they played the opening notes to Silent Night.

For no particular reason, the gorgeous old song tugged at Laura's inner waterworks. Tears tumbled from beneath her lashes and streaked down her cheeks, quickly turning cold.

She glanced away from her grandparents, not wanting them to see how quickly and thoroughly her enjoyment of the evening was dissolving.

The man to her immediate right took a step in her direction. His broad frame towered over her.

Though she had to blink rapidly to bring his features into focus, she already knew who it was. Wyatt James moved closer still to bend his head beside hers and rasp, "Are you alright, ma'am?"

She shook her head slightly, inadvertently shaking more tears loose. "I'm trying to be," she choked. It wasn't a festive answer or even a good answer, but it was the only one she could give this evening.

He produced a white handkerchief, a surprising item for a rugged blacksmith to be carrying around with him, and held it out to her.

Her gloved fingers brushed his as she accepted it. Too much emotion swelled in her throat to say more. All she could do was nod her thanks.

His gaze burned into hers as he nodded back. Awareness prickled between them again, like it had done on multiple occasions earlier.

She squeezed her eyelids shut in the effort to sever their connection. It was too powerful to fight when her eyes were open. She could still feel it when her eyes were closed. It was several moments before she could collect her emotions enough to face him again.

When she opened her eyes, Wyatt James was no longer standing beside her.

Grab your copy of
Rescuing the Blacksmith
today!

About Jovie

Jovie Grace is an Amazon bestselling author of sweet and inspirational historical romance books full of faith, family, and second chances. She also writes sweet contemporary romance as Jo Grafford.

For the most up-to-date printable list of my sweet historical books:
Click here
or go to:
https://www.jografford.com/joviegracebooks

For the most up-to-date printable list of my sweet contemporary books:
Click here
or go to:
https://www.JoGrafford.com/books

Happy reading!

Jovie